About the author

Hailing from Dehradun and presently settled in Bangalore, **Arvind Parashar** has been a corporate leader in various firms like GE, Dell and Genpact. He decided to give a break to his corporate career and pursue his passion for writing. Arvind has walked a narrow path to reach where he is today. He had to sacrifice a lot, including his job, to ensure he can chase his dream without any problems. A self-made man, today Arvind is happy that his hard work and effort are bearing fruit. His first novel was a Crossword bestseller that won many hearts. His second novel *Messed Up! But All For Love* was loved by discerning readers across the country and became one of the Amazon best reads. Not just that, this book also features in top ten best romantic thrillers by an Indian author.

Arvind is also a philanthropist and a motivational speaker. He has addressed students and corporates across the country during various sessions and literary festivals. Arvind is a crusader for education and support for intellectually disabled children. Arvind is also is a painter and enjoys painting in his spare time. He plans to do an exhibition of the same in the near future. *Lost in Love* is Arvind's third novel.

 /arvindparasharauthor
 @arvindparashar1
 @arvind.parashar
 www.arvindparashar.com

Love and Gratitude,

Praise for the book

"India's first romantic-thriller trilogy... deals with various aspects of relationships."

– The Telegraph

"Sprinkled with humour... roller-coaster ride of thrilling romance."

– The Times of India

"...draws inspiration from real life instances."

– The Hindu

"...explores new age friendships and relationships."

– Deccan Chronicle

Lost in Love

ARVIND PARASHAR

Srishti
PUBLISHERS & DISTRIBUTORS

SRISHTI PUBLISHERS & DISTRIBUTORS
Registered Office: N-16, C.R. Park
New Delhi – 110 019
Corporate Office: 212A, Peacock Lane
Shahpur Jat, New Delhi – 110 049
editorial@srishtipublishers.com

First published by
Srishti Publishers & Distributors in 2018

To my mom and dad.

Disclaimer

The book has been written in Bangalore, Mumbai, Delhi, Dehradun, Manila, on an airplane, on notebooks, a laptop and any given piece of paper and opportunity.

If you feel that some portions are better than the others, blame the location or the situation and not the writer!

Never drink and drive. Yes, you can drink and read though. Drink tea and coffee. Not alcohol.

Last but not the least, the book is not based on my life. I have imagined it all. Like I do with all my books. However, it is closer to reality. After all, even fiction is an elevated form of reality.

Possibly, it is based on yours!

Acknowledgements

Thanks for your overwhelming response to *Messed Up! But All For Love*. Now that you have read it, hope you really enjoy *Lost in Love*. This is the second of the 'Messed Up' trilogy.

Hope you know how much I love you all. I pray to God, you'd love the book so much that you talk about it with one and all.

Below are the fabulously talented women who have contributed a poem each. I thank you for the lovely work. May you go places.

Aakriti Kuntal
Dhanya Nair
Zeba Patni

Thanks so much Stuti and team for always turning my raw story into a fine novel.

Thanks to Srishti Publishers. My publishers have been extremely patient with me. I feel horrible that I delayed my manuscript submission and I promise to do a better job next time.

Jayanta da, always remember, you mean a lot to me.

Arup, thanks a lot for always being there and guiding me through the hurdles.

To my friends, family and all my fans for constantly motivating me. I owe it to you all.

Now that I have thanked one and all, you may sip your coffee or tea and lie back. Happy reading!

Special Mention

The original title of this novel was 'The Girl On My Side'. There is a small story behind the revised one. One fine day, when I was listening to one of my favourite tracks by Air Supply, 'Lost in Love', it just stayed on my lips for a long time. And then, in the course of discussions, my publishers and I felt this title is more appropriate for the book. The book is all about love. Below is the track that I mentioned above. The book does the same. Do listen in before you start reading the book.

I realize the best part of love is the thinnest slice

And it don't count for much
but I'm not letting go
I believe there's still much to believe in

So lift your eyes if you feel you can
Reach for a star and I'll show you a plan
I figured it out
What I needed was someone to show me

You know you can't fool me
I've been loving you too long
It started so easy
You want to carry on

Lost In Love and I don't know much
Was I thinking aloud and fell out of touch?
But I'm back on my feet
And eager to be what you wanted

So lift your eyes if you feel you can
Reach for a star and I'll show you a plan
I figured it out
What I needed was someone to show me

You know you can't fool me
I've been loving you too long
It started so easy
You want to carry on

You know you can't fool me
I've been loving you too long
It started so easy
You want to carry on

Now I'm lost, lost in love, lost in love, lost in love
Now I'm lost, lost in love, lost in love, lost in love
Lost in love, lost in love, lost in love
Lost in love, lost in love, lost in love

If I had my way with you, I shall turn this day into the night, let the sun go behind the moon, let the stars shine bright like never before, let the breeze turn the sound into a love song.

If I had my way, I would turn reality into a beautiful romance fiction. A story that I would read out to our grandchildren every night...night that gave our life a story to cherish.

– Arvind Parashar

Year 2001

Waiting down the choked by-lanes in the nestle and
dwellings
My heart cries out loud your name in the universe
You have vanished like there never was a thing
And I fool my soul with connivance
Kill me now O' lord if I made her trot

Gauri, my love, I call your name,
Answer now or I go insane
Your absence, the crux, that makes me fall
Return from where you've gone, for my soul weeps
My longing eyes dying to see, my skin to feel
Did I not love you enough to hold
That the reason becomes for you to be gone

Save me from drowning in the oblivion, my girl
For the seized heart utters your name
The love shall wait till eternity to unite
Or do I not deserve it any long

Cryptic appearance, delusional,
Shadows of you cross my pained eyes
I lie back here, waiting, dreading in fret and fume
I lie back here, waiting for you, and I know
Soon, soon you shall be found.

The numbness was beginning to trickle down from my head to the toe. Like you see mercury moving on the surface. It keeps breaking and moving swiftly, so did the pain inside me. I was perturbed with the situation at hand. I had to literally push my feet up and ahead to make small moves. My world had changed so much. My life had altered its course without a warning. Like it normally does. I wish it were as normal. I never had an iota of a clue that this could happen to me.

It was 7 a.m. on a monsoon morning in Pune. I was living on the second floor apartment that was a couple of kilometres from my college. Gauri was studying with me. She was two years my junior. I was pursuing my engineering and she was studying microbiology. But something unknown happened the previous evening. She did not return from the gym.

The cops had arrived in a brand new white gypsy.

"Hi, I am Inspector Vishwa and she is my colleague..." The introduction was a mere formality. He seemed to be a martinet from the very appearance of it.

"I am Senior Inspector Dhanya Nair."

"Hello, please come..." I had no better way to address them, except a normal hello. There was a tremble in my voice. I had not slept the whole night. I was alert though. I knew the process of investigation would begin with me. The questions would come my way. I was okay. The trembling could be attributed to my tired state of mind. I was not nervous. I was just shattered.

I offered hot tea to the sophisticated cops. In the rains, it made sense. I seemed to have made the first courteous move. The plain hello did not seem appropriate. This time I did add 'sir' and 'ma'am' to my conversations with them.

This year, the monsoons had struck early. Gauri and I had plans to go to Lonavala. She had turned eighteen. Few days remained to execute our travel. It wasn't my idea though. It was hers. Whenever it would be about celebrations or outings, it would be her idea. I was in love with her. It was not too deep and we were evolving in it, when we were together. But I was falling and moving in that direction before the world came crashing down. Now that she had gone missing, I felt I was already deeply in love with her. My senses were now awakened.

"So you had a tough relationship with her?"

"Please do not jump to conclusions." My eyes swirled around, with the signs of a quick shift exchanging glances with the investigators. I made my statement sound like a request.

In the middle of all this, I kept receiving calls from my mom, dad, friends, canteen wallahs, college students, union folks and also the journos. I was now getting more uncomfortable than before. It was now all sinking-in. Everyone ensured, it settles in my head that I was in for something dark and grave. No matter how hard you try to be calm in tough situations, there will be people who would rake it up so much, that you would tend to forget being normal. And most people would be your own. Like mom, dad, friends and more friends. The cops were now appearing friendly though. They insisted I take all the calls, and if need be, I could have my privacy. Who knew what their purpose was.

"Don't look hassled, Neil. It is okay. We have not even asked you the tough questions," said Dhanya. She gave a grin at the end of the conversation. Inspector Vishwa kept looking around. He kept talking incessantly though.

"What kind of a person was Gauri?"

"You mean, what kind of person *is* Gauri?"

"Yes, yes..."

"Charming, vivacious, inquisitive, detailed, a movie buff, precise... and I had only known her closely for a few weeks now."

"Is it okay then to presume you and Gauri had a short intense affair before all this happened?"

"Well, it had just begun..."

"You and Gauri were living in together, weren't you?"

"Yes, but we were not too much into each other yet. I mean she was, but I was taking my time. Like, I loved her, but was not intimate and all. I mean it was not physical." I really did not know whether I needed to say that, but I still did.

The questions stopped. The doorbell rang. Couple of guys gave a packet to Vishwa. He retained it. His hands were in his pockets now. He was an extremely alert cop who could shift gears in between. It was hard to read him. I looked at Dhanya to gain some comfort. She did not return my glances. I understood. She did not want to leave any doubt that she was my friend's fiancee. In fact, Dhanya and I had grown together, she being elder though, and I was the one who introduced her to Paul. Dhanya Nair would soon be Dhanya Paul. Gauri was on the same track. She wanted to be Gauri Bhargava. I kept thinking of her every now and then.

"Did she ask you to marry her?"

"Not directly, but she did talk about old age together."

"That is what it means, dude."

"Yes, sir."

I continued to talk. I was made to. I was asked to narrate every possible detail that I was aware of. All that had happened in the last twenty-four hours. It was step by step. Right from the morning till the time we were together. Vishwa had this habit of walking around and scanning things, while Dhanya kept sitting and looking at me. She was trying to soothe me with her expressions. She had decided that I was innocent. I presumed it based on her body language.

"Based on the CCTV footage, she was walking normally outside the gym. She carried an umbrella and crossed the street before disappearing into the non CCTV zone."

"Umbrella? Are you sure?"

"Yes, why?"

"Because, she did not carry one from the house."

"Maybe she felt it would rain, so borrowed it from someone at the gym."

"No, I can be certain. She was quite sorted in this sense. I am telling you, she always checked the weather forecast before stepping out and she knew it wouldn't rain, hence she did not carry one."

"So, you mean, she was going somewhere where she had already determined it would rain and hence... hmm.... point noted...She was carrying her usual college backpack, so no extra luggage could be seen with her...so for sure it wasn't going to be a solo holiday anywhere."

There was an awkward silence. From the discussion, it appeared that this was not an easy puzzle to solve. At least I felt so.

Vishwa spotted the post-it notes on the refrigerator.

Agatha Christie
Catch me if you can
Rains tomorrow
28 degree celsius

I explained that she was a movie buff and also into reading crime fiction. This was the reminder for me to buy her the book and download the movie. The last two were about the weather forecast.

The cops could be seen wearing a smile. After having consumed the cups of hot tea, and gathering evidences, they seemed to be working hard towards cracking the case. Dhanya noted it all, so before she allowed Vishwa to make an inference and a point, she looked at me, "She has disappeared on her own. She must have built a plot based on some Agatha novel. Therefore, only you, yes you Mr Neil, can help solve this case."

I clarified, "There is *Catch me if you can* too on the list. Does it mean she is getting a con job?"

"What if these post-its have been placed by you to misguide us?" Vishwa snapped.

I told them I had bought a new cellphone for Gauri, to gift her on our trip to Lonavala. If I had any such intention, why would I do that! I showed them the note I had written and placed inside the package.

The mystery had only begun to deepen. I was under suspicion. The cops seized the post-its and also my laptop. This was followed with a search in my house. I was taken aback. I demanded clarification. I asked if they had a search warrant. The situation suddenly turned awkward. Dhanya tried to control it and looked at Vishwa with conviction, took him aside and they talked for a few minutes. Must be a trained cop language. Dhanya did the talking after that. She was senior to Vishwa, though I had no detailed clue about their roles. She asked me not to step out of Pune. Vishwa added, "Even if you do, just keep us informed. And I am sorry for being harsh with you."

The soothing lines set my motivation levels back to how they had been, so far as my innocence was concerned. Was I a happier man? The answer was no. An obvious no.

The cops left. I was all by myself. Lost in her thoughts.

What is the common holding ground, when someone talks of the sun, moon and the stars? To a poet, it is his/her set of tools, invariably. The poet would use it mercilessly and invoke passion, love, melancholy per his or her whims and fancies. To an academician, it is a subject of study. To an astrologer, it is deep science and commercials for livelihood or a side income. Well, what does it mean for a lover? The categories of writers and artists use them a tad milder than the poets. The intent is the same. It is linked to human relationships, beauty or the scene and situation. Well, for the lover, it is a lethal combination. During love, it evokes romance, passion and happiness. More so, with the company or presence of moon and the stars. The sun is kept at bay. During the break up, the so called poets and writers give the lover enough feed to get emotional. Often times, the lover turns into a writer himself or herself and makes good use of the moon and the stars. Post break up is like post surgical care. The lover is like a patient. I had gone through this rough experience about a couple of months ago when I broke up with Arya. However, I had no inkling that I would go through a similar experience so soon. It is only worse. I missed Gauri and I missed her so bad that I couldn't have imagined. I wished I had felt so strongly when she was with me. Her absence made me believe I loved her. Truly and deeply. There was a need to confess. But then, such is life.

I was facing so much at such a young age. I really felt I was becoming a man. Until now, I believe I was a lousy young student pursuing his college degree. Playing childish pranks. Going through heartbreaks. Though I would have loved to have a natural progression. Auto transmission from a boy to man supposedly happens after marriage. I grew faster. Such disastrous circumstances are rare for any boy, in my view. I wasn't sure of the definition of a man. I was sure of the fact that nobody calls a college student a man. I was a misfit of sorts now, a slapdash amateur. At least in my head. And, when there is anything like this in your head, that only means you are thinking too hard to prove your existence to yourself.

Okay, coming to talking of being a man, my dad had always told me, a man is one who can take charge, who can take control responsibly. He would give his own examples. And in his examples, there was less space for love, and more for practicality. So he firmly believed men were practical while boys were fools, who would fall in love. By that standard, I hadn't grown up. Not a tad bit. Precisely, the cause being that I kept thinking of Gauri most of the time. I had never hurt Gauri deliberately. Conscioulsy, never. I was still reeling under my break up. I was still focusing on the moon and the stars theory of lovers, though for the first time. I was still raw. That is when Gauri had happened to me. She was madly in love with me. More madly that I could assume at that point. She wanted all of me. All of me for all of herself. In love with a twenty-year-old boy. She had followed me till college. She used to be my school junior, as I recollect all this while again. I had never paid attention to her. She had a massive crush on me. I was only focused on studies then. My dad had told me to not even think of getting close to girls. If I did, it would impact my board results. As a result of which I would not get admission in a good college and then I would end up making pizzas or burgers in fast food outlets. Cooking is something I had hated. I chose studies over girls, hence.

I had not really been able to discover Gauri fully yet. She had not given me a chance. Well, if she had disappeared intentionally and would come back and tell everyone she was only fooling around, I would completely forgive her. What happened, if she had actually been abducted. But what if she was in real trouble. Crime against women was not prevalent in Pune. Also, it was a prime location and her mobile phone could not be traced either, so it was all very deeply hidden in the dark.

I could see that my Nokia was fully charged now. I was expecting a call from my mom at any moment. She called again. This was her fifth call within the last couple of hours. She wanted to check if everything was alright. She sounded extremely worried. The reason was that Tom had forwarded all my worried texts that I had sent to him to my mom. Hell no. "Who on the earth does that, mom? How could he send those to you?"

"So, will you hide things from me now? You will tell your friends but the mother who bore you for nine months, she will not be allowed to know what is happening in her child's life?"

"Come on mom, it is fine. Don't get senti in the morning now. Where is dad?"

"Listen, dad has spoken with Jethmalani's nephew. He is a big lawyer."

'Don't tell me everyone in Jethmalani's family is a lawyer. What if he is fooling you? What if he is not his nephew?" I said with caution as I knew my parents were still those small town innocents.

"Don't you think your dad would have checked it all? And his office cabin was filled with his pics with Ram only. So you relax now. At some point, you will need a lawyer. We are with you."

"Hahahaha...Ram..hahaha...and mom, tell dad not to even think of coming down to Pune." I said, choked with laughter.

"He won't come alone. I shall come with him."

"No, you can't do that, mom!"

"Listen kid, you couldn't even handle your bestie Dhanya today. How can you handle this case?"

"Tom sent *that* text to you too?"

"Shut up now. I will talk to her when I am there. She has grown up in my lap. Did you not tell her when she was raising her voice at you?"

"No, mom. She did not. She was just doing her duty. Also, she did not want her junior to feel that she is biased."

"Grow up, Neil. Be a man. When will you talk like a man?" My father had taken the phone from my mom.

"Okay dad."

"Look, I just returned from my morning walk. The judge here in the criminal fast track court is my good friend. He only referred me to that Jethmalani chap."

"Wow dad, you have contacts!"

"I always had. I shall use them for you now. I hope this is the last time I take any obligations. You soon become a man so that in my old age, you can support us rather than us doing so."

By this time, mom had taken the phone back. My folks have always been like this. If one gets harsh or real, the other gets soft and artificial. To coax and to ease me.

"Don't mind what your dad said. He is worried for you. Don't forget to eat. Have lots of water."

The call ended finally. I am not sure if this is how it is with moms universally. Or is it like this with Indian moms only? Because in the Hollywood movies I have seen, in tough situations, moms do not ask details about food and water!

I finally lay down on the couch. I transcended into my imaginary world with two options – think like a boy or think like a man. I preferred the former. I thought of Gauri.

O my God, where have you been? Where have you ....
Will you shut up now? I was always here. I was only hiding to test your love for me.
Are you mad? Have you gone insane?
No, I am not. I kept asking you if you love me. You kept confusing me.
Of course I love you, damn it. Never do this again.
Then, never make me doubt you.

It was 9 a.m. Everybody had gone. I was trying my best to catch up on some sleep. It was the hardest thing to do today. The eyes were closed. Not that I wanted to, but they just could not remain open. After many gruelling hours of trauma and pain and meeting people, I was all by myself. I was not alone. I had Gauri in my heart and on my mind.

I held the phone in my hand
Her charming smile still ruled my wallpaper
I smiled and looked for her around me...
Alas! I sat amidst books and gift wrappers
The phone for once, beeped I thought
Fretted and perplexed; hear my heart pound
Where is my happiness which she brought
She took them all; look I'm left with a wound
The scar of my heart is deeper than oceans
The reasons unknown I seek from my phone
If only she would tell me, all her notions
I promise I wouldn't give a reason to moan.
Come back to me, my love
Cause I ain't breathing without you, my love.

It was like atom particles that you could see in your head with your eyes closed. And when those move around in trillions, you get hit hard. I realize that it was not enough for Gauri to be in my heart and mind. She had to be there physically. She was gone. What could be the worse feeling than to see the girl who was making a place in your life, suddenly gone.

Considering whatever had just happened in my interactions with the cops, the chances were that she might have been abducted. It was my preliminary conclusion. However, I needed to try hard to think of the anomalies in the past few days. For now, my brain was not working. There were tears flowing down my cheeks. I don't remember if I had troubled her to the extent that she would run away. I don't remember much about it. But I needed to try hard to think. Possibilities exist to sway the course. Nothing could be dismissed.

As I stretched my hand to wipe off my face, for a moment it felt that Gauri would sit beside me and console me. I could feel her so strongly when she was gone. I began to miss her badly when she was not around. She knew everything about me. She would keep the house in order. Perfect order. I had begun to love her. I had actually begun to feel her close to my heart. She was ruling in my senses.

The more I began to think of her, the more aloof I was becoming. I was feeling bad about myself. I was feeling weak. Whereas I should be strong and do something about it. I was not answerable to anyone, but myself.

I remembered how she had come to me once, when I was feeling low. When I was reeling under the pain of the previous break-up. It was the time when I was cribbing and sulking about Arya. When I knew the world had almost ended for me. I shuddered at the very feeling of being alone. I remember how

Gauri had held my hand that day. She had sat down. I was on the couch. Whatever she did was priceless. I did not realize its worth back then. I found it normal. I considered that it was her job as my partner to make me feel good. But I was wrong. She had a choice. She had options. She could have simply spoken from a distance, and asked me not to behave like a child. She knew me more than I had known myself. Just like my mom, she was sensitive.

Her face kept flashing across my mind. Her smile teased me to face the brutal reality that she was not around. Her charm so well contained, her poise so well defined, her beauty so ethereal, made her simply the kind of woman who deserved to have a man better than me. Any given day.

I opened my eyes to the wall clock that alarmed at noon. Time for a bath. Time for me to continue my journey into the past in the tub of hot water.

I spent a few minutes in front of the mirror. My face was horribly puffy. Like I was doing drugs. My eyes did not exist. Wrinkles did not seem to leave my forehead. I stood stiff, rinsed with some Listerine, blabbered and sank in the tub, clouded with steam. On a perfectly normal day, I would have mixed it with some cold water and made it warm and cozy. I left it hot, but did not feel the burn. All I felt was the severe pain in my chest. It was stabbing. The tears mixed well with the water, but the pain settled in. It won't go anytime soon, I knew. I laid back. Back to how it was, at the beginning of the day. Numb.

> *It all appeared to me that I was down in the drains*
> *It all seemed gone like vapours in the rains*
> *My heart and the soul not at peace*

My body detached from me not at ease
I look like a pale shallow man in the mirror
I look like I have become a man in this unforeseen horror
For my chips were down and my mind was out
I need to vent it out, I need to shout
I care for you, I love you Gauri, o my girl
Hold me back again, hold me my girl
I need you want you like never before
Come back please I would never let you go
Come back please I would never let you go.

I had to begin my thinking process again. The hot water gave me some respite and a push to gather myself.

I moved out gently and walked slowly back into the room. I appeared in my boxers and vests and sat down on the couch.

The doorbell rang. It rang a few times before I could gather my senses. I did not run to open it. I walked slowly like I had been stabbed hard. I opened it and turned back to the couch. I did not bother to find out who it was.

"What the fuck is going on, Neil?"

I was calm and quiet as Tom observed me. I was motionless and was trying to breathe in and out.

"Neil, I have got food for you. We will take care of it. You are not alone."

I have only been losing people from my life. People who have cared for me or shown concern were all leaving one by one. So I was not sure how to deal with Tom. He was my best buddy. But right now, I was vulnerable. He must have said a few more words that I could not register. I was okay to ignore those outright. Care and concern was more needed for Gauri than me, and I did not want to be further guilty of anything.

Tom began to shake me and I could feel some jerking. Within a moment, he held me tight. I had begun to howl. I was crying on his shoulders. I wept profusely. He kept moving his hands around me to console. You can never fight a battle alone. That hug from my buddy made me feel lighter. I felt better.

"Again, I repeat, you are not alone. Probably, you needed to come out with your pent up emotions."

"Tom, never leave me, bro!"

"I can't see you like this. You are the heartthrob of our college. If you don't stay strong, what will happen to the other kids out there?"

"Time to resurrect..."

"Yes, eat your food and sleep now."

"And you told mom everything, you asshole!"

"Leave that. I met Dhanya and I told her to assess it so that she can help find Gauri at the earliest."

"Yeah, she behaved erratically. I understand she was with her colleague, but still..."

"I know... she used to be on Aunty's lap when she was a kid and you have known each other since childhood."

"Hope she helps, that is all I want."

"She will. She told me she feels bad for you. In Pune, this is big news. In Delhi, this is common, so nobody pays attention. But here, she will find media and political pressure soon. It is better you get some rest so that we can meet the cops before they come knocking again."

"Yeah, bro. Sure thing. I miss her."

"I knew that when she moved in with you. I knew she had the spark. You were only reluctant to accept."

"I did not want it to be a rebound. That's all. Else, I had...."

Tom served me the food. He even cleaned my bedroom.

"Bugger, your room has so many pictures of you and Gauri together. I've seen it for the first time."

"Apparently, this is what I saw when I came back to the house."

"What do you mean? Was it not done together?"

I began to think about it. It never occured to me that way. That day, when we left for the college, these pictures were not there. That suggested Gauri had come back from college to the house and had done up the room. This was puzzling.

"Neil, I am telling you. She has been abducted. We need to tell the cops. We must!"

"Hold on! Let me get some rest. We shall talk again. Let us try to get some more clues ourselves as well."

After I had finished my food, I stretched myself and told Tom about my condition of sleeplessness. I was completely not in a mood to dose off. I kept sleep at bay. Tom was pleasantly surprised on hearing this. He knew if given an opportunity, I would sleep off standing!

"You have transformed, bro."

"I don't think so. I believe, I am too worried to even think of sleeping."

"Oh, and back then when uncle told you that there is nothing bigger than the board exams, you still slept without any revision."

"Damn! You remember that episode?"

The chatting continued in the living room. Tom kept checking the contact list on his phone, while I kept thinking of all that had happened in the past few weeks.

Suddenly, Tom came around. "Have you told Arya about this?" I was taken aback as to why would Tom even talk about her. He had never liked Arya in the first place. He considered her too flamboyant for planet earth. Nonetheless, he raised the topic.

"No, I have not told her anything. I never had time, Tom."

"Do you think we should talk to her?"

"For that matter, we should talk to the students that were common friends."

To our surprise, not many from the school had called me, except a few in the morning. But those did not include the teachers or Gauri's classmates. Gauri had a couple of friends. One was her bestie. None knew about her, or so we believed. This was another surprising element. Anyway, the cops would do their act certainly. The higher administration had been informed of the episode, but it might not have cascaded down the ranks.

The college was closed today. Even the hostelers would have stepped out, so was not sure how the investigation would proceed. We continued to grapple with these thoughts.

Before we could decide about stepping out, Arya called me. Tom noticed and looked at me with an expression that meant pointless.

I attended the call. Arya sounded concerned. I asked her how she had come to know about it. She mentioned that it was big news already. People were talking about it. I asked her to be specific. She was quiet for a while and then told me that it had been already printed in the noon daily. Also, she said it might have been broadcast on television too.

After my break up with Arya and from the time that I started seeing Gauri, there had been a big change in Arya. She was more composed, concerned and caring. She was not the Arya that I had known. I did ask her about it, and she would generally tell me that she considered me a good friend. And since we could not be great lovers, however, we could always remain good friends. Tom was pleasantly surprised and pulled me up.

"You never told me that you and Arya were still in contact."

"There was nothing to tell, bro. Nothing much."

"Well, if you add or delete a friend from your life, I assumed that I'll always be the first one to know. But in this case, you ignored me."

"Tom...relax! All of this is a recent phenomenon only."

"Yeah, your life has changed in last two or three months."

Tom was referring to my short-lived relationship with Arya, then a break up and then another one with Gauri.

Tom did not stop at that. He continued to look at me with a great deal of surprise and shock. His expressions were as if he had spotted a ghost and wondered why I was not able to see it. I further clarified. I explained again. I owed him. Friends owe each other explanations. They never draw a blank when questioned. Only after my brief spiel of conviction did he let go. The moment stopped, as Arya called up again. She wanted to visit me. Like she was vehemently concerned. She sounded perturbed. I looked at Tom, seeking his approval; he nodded in affirmation. That was all.

Tom kept looking around the house. He was in the sniffing mode. He knew I was exhausted to think or comprehend any further. Therefore he decided to find anything that the house might offer. Like anything. And he did. He spotted something that got us in a tizzy. There was a gym payment receipt in the name of Arya that was kept on the refrigerator. And I thought, if ever I had played treasure hunt to victory, I would have found it much early on.

"Look, let us not talk about this with anyone yet."

"Yeah but why did Gauri and Arya become gym partners?"

"What if they were always together in the gym?"

"Not possible, Gauri would have told me."

"But she did not..."

"Maybe she wanted to, but then somebody abducted her."

"What else do you think is possible?"

"Imagine, after my break up with Arya, Gauri and I started seeing each other. Then Arya became my friend from my ex, and now Gauri and Arya became friends."

"So in a way, your life was pretty good. No screw ups. Everything was normal. The world was the best place to be in..."

"Yeah, dog... I agree." I twitched my eyes as I was getting really tired now.

"Then, let us assume, there is something wrong. There is someone else behind this episode. We cannot rule out anything. But right now, before everything else, you must sleep."

It is a usual thing. After a sad instance in your life, you are alone at first, then you have people all around you and then when they're all are gone, you feel more alone. There is a kind of vacuum that gets created. A point comes when you are lost. That is when the weirdness begins to sink in. The negative surrealism captivates you. You begin to rewind on the instances that had happened to you. They strike you. I was now comprehending what was happening to me. The ordeal in the sapping twenty hours had shrouded my senses. My eyes bled red. I could feel the burn in them. I wanted to ease out a bit. I wanted to relax a bit. I wanted to relax to the point of sleeping. It would not come till the thoughts stopped haunting my active mind.

It was about a month ago that I had rammed into Gauri. In our college library. Not like filmy stuff. Because in the films, the books fall down. Mostly, it is the girl who is holding the books. The guy bends down to lift them up. Nothing of this sort happened. She and I had known each other. My knowledge about her was faint and vague, while in her case, it was different. Since our school days, she was infatuated on me. She loved everything about me. So, when I rammed into her, she simply held my hand. I was on the bounce back from my break up. She tightened the grip. I smiled. She hugged and whispered something I could not understand.

"Sorry, Gauri. I could not understand what you just whispered in my ears."

Some love stories begin with a crush. Often, boys have a crush on a girl and sometimes, it is the other way round too. Those are love stories as well. The so-called one sided love stories. Not necessarily revealed to each other. So, as far as love is concerned, it grows in the physical presence. It can also be fatal attraction. Or conversely, this could be a two-sided love story. Most of the college juniors were aware of Gauri's attraction for me. To the extent that Gauri decided to leave the beautiful Guwahati city after schooling for me. And she had decided to join my college. While I studied B.Tech, she pursued microbiology. The science of the subjects remained common between us. Everything else might not have been as common. I had slightly known Gauri as my junior. To me, when I had rammed into her in the library, it seemed like a mere coincidence. Well, honestly, that is how we reacted. Or maybe I did not pay attention. Maybe she did not let me pay much attention. This was ten days after my break up with the adventurous Arya.

Gauri did not lose the opportunity of using the right set of words then. Words that would melt me.

"I understand what you are going through."

I was taken aback at first. How would she know what I was going through? But more than that, why would she not say hello. Why would she just strike the bottom of my heart that was wounded. Why would she offer an immediate healing touch. Maybe she had said hello to me and I had not heard her or it was not said aloud and she did not realize it out of nervous anxiety. I only briefly saw her cheeks turn pink. That was it. As she got conscious by now, she greeted me. I did not react much, as she was junior to me, who had had a soft corner for me in school. However, she was not like any other girl. It was probably the first time I saw her so close. She did too. It was the first time I had heard her voice so clearly. Back in school, it was heard only during the choirs, school parade or recess screams of raucous students. In the past, her voice was never singled out. Now, it sounded catchy. It was sugar sweet. I doubted if I could forget her voice anytime soon. A voice that comes straight from the heart and hits yours can never be forgotten.

That five-minute conversation in the library was imbalanced, for she spoke for four minutes and I did my bit in one. That is how it started finally.

"Oh my god! Is that you, Neil?"

"Hell, yes, you recognize me?"

"Of course. Two years only...away from you. And you were the head boy. The dashing head boy."

I was seemingly flattered. The entire twelfth class flashed before my eyes. I remembered her.

"I recognize you. Gauri, right?"

"I can't believe you remember my name."

"Who can forget the charming basket ball captain of class X?"

The conversation took us to the college amphitheater. What started from the library as a five-minute coincidental face time turned into a long chat. Another thirty minutes spent together. She spoke for twenty-six and I got my four minutes back here. This was a nice ice-breaker for me. So when I asked her how she felt after talking to me, she was ready, as though she was waiting for me to ask her that,

"You are my first casual date."

"Oh wow! I mean, really?"

"Yes, and before you jump the guns, you are the first guy whom I have spoken to at length."

"And then, you still think you understand what I am going through."

Thereafter, Gauri kept talking. She wouldn't stop. She spoke for good fifteen minutes. It appeared that she had been waiting for her meeting with me.

"So, Neil. Imagine there is someone I love. One-sided. And I have loved him for the last seven years. All one sided. I never told him till date."

"You are unique, aren't you?"

"Of course, how many people have you heard of being in love for seven years and that too one-sided?"

"I think it is one-sided and hence it lasted seven years. If it were two-sided, it might have been a story similar to mine."

"Nobody will know till you get into it."

"But why did you not tell him about it?"

"My mom wanted me to turn eighteen before confiding in anyone in case I was in love. She said I needed to be an adult before approaching the guy."

"Why?"

"So that if my parents didn't approve of him, I was at the right age to run away."

I could not stop laughing. I liked the way Gauri spoke. She was certainly different. I was still trying to understand her. Though we got off to a lot of personal discussion, I still did not ask her much about the person she loved. I thought maybe she would do it on her own. But she did not. So I decided to break the conversation in such a manner that it ended up having her respond to me. I thought if the girl is being so nice to me, I can be of some help to her. Maybe I can get her to meet the guy. Well, I was not that naive, I knew what she meant. But I had to carry that innocent ignorance charm.

"I can understand what you are going through."

"Aha! You are smart Neil. Handsome Neil."

"Thanks for that. Not as good as you though."

"Well, thanks. If I were actually smart, I would have been real bold in confiding my feelings in the person. I tend to be shy."

"That's not fair for the guy. Maybe, the guy is missing out on being with such a uniquely smart and beautiful woman like you."

"Hmm. Yes that is correct. I believe we should leave now. I have my next lecture coming up."

"Sure thing. Hope to see you soon."

"Do come for dinner tomorrow."

"What is the occasion?"

"Well, I am turning eighteen. Finally."

"Wow, happy birthday in advance."

I was so intrigued by the way Gauri led the entire conversation. She was sophisticated. Mature. Balanced. Loving. That is what I could gather in those forty-five minutes. More than anything else, she was witty and straightforward.

It was a bright sunny day. The air carried a bit of moisture indicating a probable shower in the evening.

I called her up to confirm the time. She told me it was 7 p.m. Also she cautioned me that it would rain around that time, so I should come early to avoid a traffic jam. I honoured her word and arrived at her place at sharp 7. She and her friend Itishree welcomed me warmly. Gauri appeared and sat with me. She asked me everything about Arya. I opened up to her with ease. I began to talk about my life with Arya. My brief spell of a relationship with her.

❖

Arya was the first girl who had happened to me. We were together for nearly three months. Short enough to call it a relationship. Those three months were mostly like a dream. Fantasy in the true sense of the word. Barring a few days that were not so great, rest was life.

The girl was madly in love with me. It was fun. Fun that you have in college. I was supposed to be in the hostel. However, our love life led me to rent an apartment so we could live in together. I could remember my conversations with Arya.

"I love the place, Neil."

"I love the fact that you love it."

"I love the place because it will have you and I in it."

Arya and I have been ultra romantic. While I got the place, Arya got the decor. I got the stuff and she put it to use. Just like life. We had a life that we were excitedly looking forward to. She gave it meaning. We were called a bomb couple in our college. Arya was not a normal girl. She always said any life below ordinary ain't worth loving. She lived up to it. It was a perfect start. To an imperfect jolted ending. It started with coffee and ended with vodka shots. It started with 'Nothing's gonna change my love for you' and ended with 'It must have been love'. Melodramatic indeed.

3 months ago

We enjoyed getting drenched in the rains together. It was after our college fest once that we decided to go for a drive to Lonavala. That was probably the first time I would have felt love in my skin. The two of us left in my brand new Hyundai Santro. 'Hysteria' was just the perfect song. I began to sing my own version of it. The winds added a chill. I parked the car on the shoulder. We stepped out.

Come near, too close, I want your over dose
Come here, too near, I want to feel you dear
Hold me, wrap me, let the rain weave the magic around
Come near, come close, you are my soul that I have found
This rain is singing to me, this rain is driving me mad
This rain is doing me up, getting the best of this lad
It is hysteria when you are near...

And she would say nothing to my version of love. She would only hold me tighter. She was getting firmer. The rain has some magic. At twenty, it makes you feel like a man. At twenty, on the highway, when a woman holds you in the broad daylight, getting drenched, it makes you feel like a man.

"You complete me."

"I feel you."

"You make me go crazy."

"I can feel your hear beat."

"I wish this could go on forever, Neil."

"I love the way you look in the rain."

It was our own lines, in our own ways, with no response to what we asked. This was focus. We were focused on each other. Completely. I was into her like she was into me.

I had began to kiss her. She continued to fondle and caress me before we decided to get back into the car. 'Two steps behind' played now. I was no more lost in the lyrics, but I could, in my faded senses, feel the music, to the point of keeping me excited.

The clothes were thrown onto the back seat. The car indicator was turned on. It never bothered us, the vehicles passing by. Arya had pink nipples. Those were hard. The water dropped down her body and I kept licking it along her skin. She looked gorgeous. She looked astonishing in her skin. It was the first time I felt the complete touch of a woman. It was actually the first time I was all set to make love. Maiden love. We were making love in the front seat. Reclined completely. The door was open. My legs were out. Hers were stretched down the front dashboard. The kisses and licking continued. It had turned dark by now. I did not realize that Arya had scratched my back to the extent of peeling the skin off. She could not resist the pleasure of making love to me. Within sometime, she was completely lying back. Her legs were open. Now she kept holding me slowly and kept moving her hands on my shoulders and back. I was completely inside her. She was wet and I was hard. The water kept sprinkling on our bodies. She asked me to push it fast. I ejaculated on her breasts. We hugged tight. We continued to smell each other's skin while feeling it. Then we looked into each other's eyes with that warmth and appeal. She kissed my lips again. It was a quiet moment of love. Magical. Surreal. We did not want to let it go. Then we were out, to get wet and cleaned up in the rain. It was no less than a perfect fantasy. We lived it for real. It was bold and adventurous. It was love. Absolute love.

Whoever would have thought or felt that you lose sense in the act of making love when you are actually in love, is right. You lose every bit of it. We were completely addicted to each other. She said towards the end, "I cannot live without you."

We had struck off quite early in our relationship. We got intimate without giving much time to each other. Our contrary personalities did not seem to matter. I still remember how I had told her once, that even if I saw Miss World, I would not be able to fantasize about her. I believe that is a normal thing for a boy to feel when he is mad for a girl. He cannot think about anyone else. Even in his dreams. For a woman, it is considered to be a default setting. They rarely cheat. That's the worldview too. I stand by it. I never cheated or would cheat either. That remains a fact.

If I sum up my life with Arya, it would be safe to say that I never wanted to leave her. She had something about her that made her irresistible. She was perfect. She was, in fact, a perfect girl. Well, she was overtly flamboyant. She was an extrovert. She was a freak. She was an adventure. She was an animal. She had everything that I had lacked. She was looking for a single malt in gin. She was looking for cheese in raw cream. I was an unfinished product.

I never realized that I had shortcomings. She never told me so. I could assume based on my judgement and the sequence of events. She left me abruptly without a warning. She just did not leave me, she dumped me. Who leaves anyone, so soon, after only a few days of steamy sex? It was unbelievable.

What irked her? What was ailing her? Was she not normal? What was her true definition of being extraordinary? The questions hit me hard later.

The next day, we went to hit the local pub. Loved the music. It was the party culture that could be witnessed out there. I was high and so was Arya.

Come on now get me groovin'
Come on now get me pumpin'
How about a twistin'
How about some spinnin'
Get me on get me on now
Let the beats, set you movin'
Let the music get you goin'
Tonight we groove, set us on fire
Tonight we move, fill my desire
Come on now, get me movin'
Come on now, get me groovin'
Come on come on let's get it on
Come on come on let's set it on
How about some shakin'

How about we makin'
Let's do it let's make some love
Let's shake it let's shake some more
Oooo' Oooo' let's do it...
Come on come on let's do it...

I knew my songs always turned Arya on to the deepest sensuality levels. She got so high on music and the lyrics that she pulled me aside and kissed me hard. We did not spend much time out there.

We returned to my apartment. It was all about removing our clothes and slipping between the sheets. The night lamp was also turned off. We wanted to do it in pitch dark. Like we wanted to just go wild. No observations needed. No desire to see each other's body. Only to feel it. See it through the darkness. Darkness has enough light when the souls are illuminated. So we did not feel the need for it. What appeared to be a feeling, now seemed to have elevated to be an artwork. Love making is indeed one hell of an artwork.

All went fine. However, too much too soon isn't good. Life in a fast lane comes to a halt too. I was actually not an adventure freak. I wasn't the one who would hang out. That was not my default setting. That is why we had different personalities. I was still pretending and doing so. I would ram into a girl, yet be without a reaction. I was that sort. So all my adventures that started with Arya were more or less temporary. She did know it. Like I said, it all happened too fast. So, whenever I would refuse to hang out, she wouldn't like it. Often, it invited her wrath. Now that is sometimes common with couples. Especially with the newbies. The ones who are just starting off. They are abrasive. I was calm though. She would keep showing deep dark secrets of her negative emotions to me. She behaved like a man – a wild man. I was always the boy. We were on the decline. The love was slowly fizzing out. The bubble was about to burst.

The worst was when she had planned a complete surprise for me. A weekend-getaway to Mahabaleshwar. I was supposed to prepare for my debate. It was a matter of confilct between an inter college debate versus Mahabaleshwar. It was institution versus love. Dignity versus love. But most of all, it was me versus her. The discussion began on Thursday evening 5 p.m.

"Neil, you have fucked up so many times in the past couple of weeks. No to my favorite movie. No to Riya's party. Now, I had planned this and you...."

"Hmm..."

"What is hmm? Will you fuckin' say anything?"

"Well...."

"Now, do you even think you are in any state to say anything?"

"Look, Arya baby, you have to understand..."

"Wow, Neil...wow...you have the audacity to speak and tell me it is a problem with my understanding."

"Look, I am sorry."

"Does it help?"

"What do you want?"

"Nothing."

The time that a person can give as an option was lost. It was more like a psychological test. She could have said yes and something towards the end. But she refused to do so. She had been already rejected once. So she did not want to get rejected again. In this scenario, if I had said no, which she assumed I would, things wouldn't have been fine. Anyway, I just said yes and she said no. Things changed. Things kept changing thereafter. But it was all happening way too fast. Similar to the way we fell in love. And now, we were falling apart. Maybe I was over-thinking. Not yet. Not at this stage. I wasn't sure. That night, Arya cried a hell lot. She was not the wild man in this relationship. She was probably still a teenager who would behave like one. The case was simple. A boy had to handle a teenage girl. There was no book that guided one so. Everything was supposed to be meant for men and women. Nothing ever said that girls were from Venus. It was only when they become women do they evolve from the planet. They are somewhere else as a girl. So my life was shitty. Scary, because things were to break now. I was brooding.

Arya reported that she was down with fever the next morning. I showed my concern. Made her some soup. Then offered her tea. She remained quiet and thanked me each time I did something for her. She refused to see the doctor, no matter how much I insisted. Thereafter, I stepped out to get a doctor's appointment. I returned after an hour. She was not at home. She was gone. She left a note on the dining table.

Dear Neil,

I did not want to leave you this way, but my fever has done something to my body that I am compelled to leave you like this.

I shall be fine. I doubt if we can ever get back to each other. I wish to move on and hope we have a great life ahead.

With love,
A

Wow, she has dumped me with love, I said to myself. I said many things to her in my head and kind of felt weird. The feeling was yet to sink in. Whatever it was, I was not okay. I wanted to get in touch with her, however the letter kept flashing across my eyes. I was hurt. Deeply. I was sad. Extremely. I was lost in love. I was lonely. The feeling was indescribable. I agonise the time when we were setting ourselves to ending our relationship. That was tormenting. The only way forward for me was to fall in love with myself. I had rarely done that before. I think that would be a perfect start.

Back in the present moment, Gauri kept her hand on my shoulders and said, "Come on, you have had enough. No more sulking. Hope you only have happiness forward."

I looked at her and wondered how.

Suddenly, there was a lot of noise and everybody pulled Gauri aside. There was a cake to be cut. I kept sitting at my position. I was thinking. I could hear Gauri screaming my name and asking me to come by her side. I obliged. What happened after birthday greetings was like a sweet surrender.

"I've turned eighteen. I love you. I wish for you to fall in love with me."

I turned red within a jiffy. She hugged me. Everything was spoken via the eyes thereafter. And some smiles.

Five days went by. We continued to talk and meet up in the canteen. Amongst several other love birds. Mine for sure was not a love story yet. It was forming beautifully though.

Day 6 of my new beginning

The phone buzzed. I had put a different ringtone for her. It was this song, 'Lost in Love' by Air Supply. In fact, that was both ring tone and the caller tune on my phone. So, Gauri and I were effectively listening to the same song. That is how I was building my connection with my new girl. Music connected us. Like it connects the souls. Cliché. More or less. What else do you expect from a twenty-year-old boy? Heartbroken and taken again now.

"Hi Neil, sorry if I woke you up on a Saturday."

"Nah! The sun already did. Bright things waking me up is the order of the day."

"So, you mean I am bright?"

"You are brighter. You are God's astonishing act of saving me."

"Did I save you from the claws of break up and depression?"

"Much more than that."

"In time…hmm…what's the plan?"

"You want to come over?"

"Open the door," she said wittingly.

I jumped and flew to the knob. She actually shone brighter than the morning sun, waiting to cheer me up. Within two minutes of her entry, the world changed inside the house. The clothes were all well shoved inside the almirah. The shoes flipped across and made their way below the bedside table. The shoe rack was supposedly used for keeping empty kingfisher bottles and the newly introduced cans that we got from Richie Rich shop, exclusively meant for imported stuff. Thankfully, no weed or pot or Manala crème. That reminded me to put Manala village in my bucket list. I had heard so much about it. Amsterdam of India.

I could hear the doorbell fading away. I was in my imagination. Now I was significantly back in my world. I shook myself and staggered towards the door, like I was already delayed.

"Looks like I got you at the wrong time."

"Yeah, like you woke me up." I looked at her and she was exactly like I was thinking. She was shining bright.

"Aha! So the truth touched your lips."

"Sarcasm…humour…"

"Blame it on the figure of speech."

"I have been waiting for you."

"Hence it took you thirty minutes to open the door. Huh!"

"Fuck! Really… that damn Manala thingi."

"What about that? By the way, you have really kept your house in order. Tough to expect it from a bachelor. Or does someone else live with you?"

"What nonsense?"

"Sarcasm...humour...mister...*samjhe*?"

I did not realize how comfortable I had become with Gauri so soon. It kind of took off with ease. My mind that seemed ransacked was coming to terms with normality.

"So, I was thinking...based on our humour and sarcasm match, we should plan a trip to Himachal."

"Be precise."

"Manala... umm...heard it is ..."

"The Amsterdam of India."

"You know it?"

"My bestie's maternal uncle lives there. Well not exactly Manala, but Shimla."

"Itishree?"

"Yes. Iti."

It had begun to pour now. It is a necessity to have rains in this situation. How else will our small little world form? And then, all that I could think of was the rainbow outside my window. The drizzle caressing the air and rain speckled windows calling you near. The leaves rustling through the breeze. The twigs falling between the rainbow and the streaks of water falling between the view. It was panoramic, what made it more beautiful was the way the sun rays made a crystal like appearance between the glistening water drops. Well, what made it the most beautiful was the companion alongside.

"You know there are going to be thunderstorms and torrential rains tonight."

"Then, what happens to our plan?"

"The weekend expires tomorrow. It will be a bright day. We can do that tomorrow, can't we?"

"Okay, then let me call Tom in the evening."

"Sure, I shall have Iti join us too. We are on day six together and I love it."

She remembered everything. And she was precise, I thought.

"I love it too, Gauri," I said, after a careful observation of my new love-to-be. The lovely plan with awesome friends would wrap up our Saturday night. It was the second Saturday of the month and our college was off. It was only about a week together, and Gauri wanted it to be for a lifetime, while I was almost getting in sync with her.

"Hope this lasts forever," I quipped.

"I shall last as long as you," she smiled.

Weather brings people closer, I noticed that. At the same time, I remembered how it was all fine in that rain with Arya, but I was dumped. I did not want to be burdened with the past baggage, however I did not have that luxury yet. It would take some time for me to erase her. I knew Gauri would give her best. But I did not want to share much of my fears with her. Fear of losing. Fear of being used. Fear of everything including the unknown. It wasn't easy to be in my shoes. And I wasn't willing to imagine what it would be like for Gauri. I was concerned for myself.

"Neil, you seem preoccupied. I served you coffee like twice now. Are you okay?"

"Oh, I am so sorry. Yeah, I am fine. Just thinking of my mom," I fumbled.

"I remember her from the school days."

"You seem to remember everything about me."

"You shall discover it all in time, my Neil."

That was the line of comfort, belonging and a kind of love note. She called me hers. My heart had begun to simply skip the beats. I was in the interim, studying her expressions further. I always loved it. That gave me an opportunity to ceaselessly look at her. She sat beside me on the couch. Her lap on mine, and knees tucked in. My racing heart made me take a step. I held her hand and wrapped it in mine. I kept kissing her knuckles. She did not resist. My heart was making me take these bold steps. Day six and I was extremely close to her. The coffee turned cold again. I did not realize it. Gauri did.

"Gauri, are you always like this? I mean, thoughtful and a romantic soul?"

"Yeah, if making coffee a few times makes me romantic, then I am par excellence."

"Damn you!" I laughed within myself.

I felt like I was sitting by the seaside. Those glassy sea waves and the sound of them were a dreamy affair. The calmness of the moon and the beauty of the twinkling stars added to the fantasy. It was not the rain's effect, it was Gauri's.

For so much of love and care that I could feel, I wrote a few lines and immediately recited them to Gauri.

The thorns live by the rose and yet embrace
The dignity and character remains unfazed
The power of us and the magic of your love
Is dignified like the rose and thorns in embrace.

The reaction was unexpected. She had tears rolling down her cheeks even before I could complete my lines. She jumped on me and could not stop hugging me. Before I could speak further, she put her fingers on my lips, asking me to stay shut. She curled herself on my lap. That moment, I simply loved. I was soaked in love. I was drenched in love. I was falling in love.

"If I were to ask you something right now, would you deny it?" she asked.

"Ask anything and I shall be grateful to you."

"I shall be elated if you allow me a place in your house?" she said with a slight hesitation.

"Live-in? Are you sure?"

"Yes. I want to feel I am on the moon, so please accept."

"Isn't that too soon?" I was not yet out of the previous heartbreak and this sounded too soon, so thought of confirming.

"Seven years and six days, Neil. I fell for you on my eleventh birthday. Now tell me if that is so soon."

"Oh, that is a long time, I agree. So you are convinced."

"Are you considering or agreeing completely?" she said with a glint in her eyes.

"I am completely smitten with you and would not give it anything but my complete faith," I said with an unbelievable expression.

She came closer to me and put her mouth almost in my ears, "Thank you, my Neil."

This was not planned. This was destined. Every time she spoke, it was taking my heartbeat away. I completely deafened to the sound of rain pouring outside. It was the calmness of the sea now. At this point, I was not insecure, nor did I fear losing her. Rather, my belief in love strengthened. At this point, my belief in destiny proved beyond merit.

Gauri trusted her instincts more than anything else. That is why she was always confident when it came to me and her. She had everything packed already. It was in her car. All she had to do was to hand over the keys to me. I could not understand it at first.

"There isn't much. Just a couple of bag packs and a large stroller. Everything else will be managed by Iti."

"What! You kidding me? You moved with your paraphernalia already."

"Yes. I am aware that parking my car is a problem as you only have one space. But don't worry. Iti will take it. However, you have two bedrooms, so that will fit me fine," she said breathlessly. That is how my life with Gauri was shaping. Peculiar and also a bit adventurous in the positive sense. I was participating in the actions with her. She wasn't making me do so. I was doing it with ease and happiness and all my willingness.

"Listen, are you up to some games?"

"You mean, love games?"

"Haha. No...simple stuff. I will explain it to you. It is fun. While I do so, could we have some music, Neil? Let me turn this television off."

"Sure, let me play some. What else?"

"Then we will watch a movie in the evening."

I could not hear what Gauri had said as I was downstairs, getting her stuff from the car. Books and movies formed an essential part of the lot. In fact, that consisted most of the luggage in white covered bags. The guards smiled at me, like they would when they see that a young chap had found a new girlfriend who was also moving in. Thankfully, Pune was open to these ideas. If it were Guwahati, I would have been royally screwed by everyone. I was still the only one in my friends circle and in my family too who would have dared to repeat this act. I was certain, in my family, many of them would have tried or maybe were doing it secretly, however nobody ever confided in me. Not even my elder cousins. All the younger ones were still in school. Maybe they were also going through the same crush phase that Gauri had been in for a long period. I have stories forming in my life. Stories of life in Pune and live in with a childhood 'crusher'. Crusher, as she had a crush on me. There I go!

I was pleasantly surprised to see the house in order. It was never like this before. I figured my shoes weren't that old as they appeared before. The refrigerator also needed no replacement. All was done in fifteen minutes.

"Are you a wonder girl?"

"Yeah, heavily inspired by that television series...you remember that name? Damn! how could I forget. Anyway, leave that! By the way, I have been working on it intermittently ever since I arrived. Seems you observed it just now...."

"True, as I was busy looking at you."

"Listen, hope you are not flirting with me."

"Even if I am, I shall always be with you."

"I love you for this, Neil. Hey, how about watching *Casablanca* in the afternoon?"

"That's a brilliant black and white idea."

"You are a sweetheart."

While she was talking, she had designated a place for everything around the house. What goes where had all her control now. Including my room. She set my room in order, followed by hers and the attic and the washrooms and the kitchen. The entire house was done in no time. I was astounded. I was flabbergasted. I wondered what an energy reserve she possesed. What a wonderful human being she was, that I could not even imagine in my dreams.

A human is known by karma and not the skin they wear. It is one's karma eventually that makes people love each other more. You cannot fall in love by the definition of it. It is the human's deeds that strengthens your position in his or her life. Initially it could be like love for your smile or your face or the way you talk or anything else. Mostly, it concerns the physical aspects. Thereafter, reality sinks in. Karma takes over. Love is a subset of it. It is an amalgamation of trust, care, understanding and several such variables. So by that logic, karma is huge. It is far bigger than just love. Gauri was doing great karma. Well sorted. So she was far superior than me. She was much more than I could have envisaged.

That is how it started with her. From the school time crush to college chats to love and live in. And now everything was moving together.

"Which part do you enjoy in *Casablanca*?"

"All of it."

"Aha!"

"Yes, it is like you asking me what do I love about you."

"And you love me...all of me?" she asked with a smile.

"I believe so."

"Sometimes, I find it surreal that you say words that are so powerful that I find it hard to believe how you are so perfect with your words."

"Wish I could define it. But all the variables of love have been checked out as positive for you and me."

"Thanks, my Neil. I shall remember your analysis."

"And I shall remember your karma and precision."

Casablanca had this magical effect on me. I know it was a doomed romance, yet it was so deeply etched in my head.

"*You know how you sound? Like a man who's trying to convince himself of something he doesn't believe in his heart.*"

"Oh my God, you remember the lines so perfectly well."

"*When it comes to women, you are a true democrat.*"

"Gauri, I cannot believe you know it all. *Welcome back to the fight. This time I know our side will win.*"

"Aha! You remember too, Neil. How about a game in real? "

Gauri was tempted into playing a game after my lines inspired her. A game that I had never heard of before. It was called the game of obfee. Basically shortened from object and feeling. In the game, there are ten objects. Those need to be picked by each of us, one at a time. The act needs to follow what the object suggests. It could be anything that you believe it suggests, till such time you are able to explain it to the opponent. However, the act needs to be relevant. And the act needs to invoke a feeling. The feeling could be love, hatred, fear, sadness, laughter or anything.

It appeared tough at first. Gauri decided to put ten objects of her choice. I assumed it was random. She wanted to pick the first object so that it helped me understand the game objectively.

"Look, whatever I pick, that shall be my object. I cannot look at this basket while picking, so I have to keep my eyes closed. I cannot feel the object. You spin the basket and whatever I touch at first is mine. And then I can ask you to do anything that eventually will lead you to understand the game. Whosoever wins can ask the opponent for anything. I mean anything."

"What! You are scaring me now."

"Wait, it is fun."

"So here I go...umm...are you done spinning or shuffling?"

"Yes, G. Pick it."

"What did I get? Aha....that's an easy one. A Cadbury's chocolate bar."

She pulled it out. She went to the kitchen and warmed it a bit. Took a bite. Molten around her lips and stepped back. Danced and sang out a song to me. That cadbury's song:

Kuchh khas hai, hum sabhee mein,
Kucch baat hai hum sabhee mein,
Baat hai, khaas, kuchh swad hai,
Kya swad hai zindagi mein...

Then she came closer to me and held my hand. I felt loved.

"Tell me what you feel."

"I feel loved."

"See I told you, it is simple. Now your turn..."

We enjoyed the game thoroughly. So far, she was winning. As I did not know what to do with the chips, except eating. The last one was a Hide and Seek cookies pack. She literally played the game. She went hiding. I could not find her. She had won already. By a huge margin. Like 5-2. But then, I got scared. It had been more than fifteen minutes. I was not able to trace Gauri.

"Where are you? I have lost you. I think you are here. Come on Gauri...don't scare me."

She jumped out from right behind me. I could not believe she was so near and I could not find her. I was scared at first and now I was kind of upset with her. I wanted to control myself, but I could not.

"This is the last time, Gauri. Never do this with me."

"Oh, come on, why are you so serious? It is just a game."

"Yes, for you, but for me...no..."

"What the fuck are you talking about? Hide and seek is an age-old game that all kids have played. Why are you getting worked up?"

"Maybe I should not...okay...sorry."

She was quiet. She was facing the other side. I was sitting on the couch. There was pin drop silence. Silence that can kill you if it lasts beyond a few minutes. So I took the first step and hugged her from behind. I could hear the silent tears. I turned her around.

"Oh hell. Why are you crying? It was nothing big."

She remained quiet. Then after a momentary pause, she spoke softly. I had to literally get closer to her face to hear her. Like real close.

"I am sorry," she said laughing and crying.

This was our first couple kind of ice-breaker. This was not part of the game. But all the emotions burst out in one.

"So, Gauri, does it mean that is an equalizer? In this game, I made you hide, laugh, cry, sad and all the relevant stuff you mentioned."

"Shut up now! I had won long ago."

"Okay, you win."

"Thank you. I shall ask you what I demand, in time."

"You deserve it all."

Interestingly, in my view, based on my life experience so far, love and the life of a human has ten aspects of love. For the benefit of understanding, let us call it a stage, though it is not in any perfect order, yet placed in the most relevant way.

Stage 1   –   love at first sight.

Stage 2   –   proposal for a relationship (we are not talking of rejections here).

Stage 3   –   Act of building a life together.

Stage 4   –   Movies, drives, food, talks, late night talks, early morning talks, 24/7 talks.

This is the best stage. Though this can be testing too. All the emotions and feelings come alive at this stage. You love it, as you are exploring each other. And one wishes, the world of the couple stops at this stage. The stupid stuff comes after this.

Commitment. Proposal for a live in or marriage.

Stage 5 – Parents feature.

Stage 6 – Fights, love, fights, love. Drama basically.

Stage 7 – Break up or marriage.

Stage 8 – Break up after marriage or life continues happily or sadly. Life continues.

Stage 9 – Kids. More kids. Or re-marriage and repetition of Stage 1-7 or 8.

Stage 10 – Which is like anything between Stage 1 and 2 or before 1, when you remain single. Rarely. Because human beings don't learn and life continues to teach them. The reason I have put this in the last is to let you make it flexible and put any add ons here.

One thing I can assure you is that your life shall come across more than one stage at least. Thrilling, isn't it? At 20, if I am making such predictions, you've got to give me some credit. When I turn 40, I may look back and laugh at my analysis. Who knows what lies in the store? Anyway, I was cherishing my present moment.

"Yes I deserve it all, because I deserve you more than anything else," she replied with a broad smile.

It was the evening. We were waiting for Tom and Itishree to join us. The preparations were all intact. The house was more like a home. The home was smiling and feeling the beauty of the lovely humans that were now a part of it. It felt amazing. More amazing after that small little fight and make up. More amazing after I found her back in the game. More amazing after losing to her. I don't mind losing to her a million times in any game. That was instinctive. That was driven by my chain of thoughts. Nope. That was purely driven by my heart. Hence the instinct. So I stand corrected.

"Neil, remember I told you early on that I shall last as long as you?"

"Yes, I do, G."

"Slight correction. I shall last forever."

I embraced Gauri. I held her close and gently whispered in her ears, "I shall last as long as you, my Gauri."

I could notice that she was moved, as she immediately knocked on the wood. Literally.

Love was beginning to seep in. It is not that I did not think of going beyond just holding Gauri. It is not that I did not think of kissing her lips. It is not that I did not think of kissing her all over. I did that a few times over. Every time the thought of getting intimate with Gauri struck my mind, I retracted from that thought. It was a weird thing to do, but I did. I felt that if at this stage, which is quite early in our relationship, I took that step, then it would mar our bond. I just thought like that. Now when Gauri had begun to trust me, it made all the more sense for me to let it develop and nurture and mature. That was the path I was taking. I was happy about it. I did not mention that to Gauri. Just kept it within me.

The last rays of the sun had begun to fade away. It was not as bright anyway for the last half an hour. The rains had stopped after creating some elements of romance in the air. The palm trees held on to the rain drops in its dwelling, like the clouds hold water. And then they would begin to fall off the greens. It was magnificent. To normal people, the world outside had become normal too. It was a nice spell. I caressed the breeze, kissed the miniscule droplets that were falling from the still sky. I observed the palm in greater detail. I talked to it. This time around, the winds interfered in my romance with the palm. It was more like music being added to my day's activity.

"Look, who is here!"

"Damn! When did you guys come?"

"I kept asking you to open the door, but you seemed lost. In the weather, I suppose."

"Darn! This lovely weather will kill me." I hugged Tom and Itishree.

"By the way, did you guys come together?"

"Nah! Arrey, I came in an auto and Tom brought his bike. Just that we came up together. Coincidentally."

"Itishree, you almost sound like Gauri," I said.

"Friends for sixteen years now. It is the effect of togetherness."

"That's longer than me and Neil. We know each other for about a decade now. And we sound different."

"And behave differently too."

"Or maybe it only holds true for women?"

"Well, I know that when a man and woman live together, they take each other's attributes."

The girls automatically withdrew themselves from the conversation. They kept talking in each other's ears. I could not hear them. I was kind of certain that Itishree must be asking Gauri about me. I did not realize or think consciously that I was looking at them both. Like I wanted to be a part of the discussion. Then I remember what I had been told by my mom once. Never eavesdrop when two girls talk. No matter who they are. Well, it was not because my mom was trying to teach me some respect or manners. It was not the case at all. What she had meant was that it is a frivolous effort to overhear any woman's conversation. Because, if it was pertaining to you or sounded spicy to you, then eventually it would hit your ears. It wouldn't remain a secret. I remembered that, but I still kept looking at them, like I had lost my track completely. Tom nudged and alerted me. I turned around as if nothing had happened. Tom and I went to the balcony. That was a better idea. Let the girls be at peace. We continued to talk and the women joined us a little later.

"Boys, what are you doing all by yourselves? We are here too. Why didn't you call us?"

"Come on, you were busy talking."

"Like we were discussing secret defence deals that you could not interrupt."

"Haha. Come na, join us now."

Itishree stood there while Gauri stepped inside. Tom went in to help her. Itishree and I started off with a casual conversation. She was a pleasant girl to talk to. I hadn't got much chance to interact with her on Gauri's birthday.

"So, we were talking about you."

'Holy cow,' I said to myself.

"I thought so."

"So you were watching us, haan?"

"No, I was waiting for you both to shut up, so I could invite you to the balcony."

"Aha! Precisely why Gauri was talking so highly of you. She has been head over heels over you for so many years. But I see her more composed now. Ever since you have accepted her proposal, she is so content. She is ...."

"Listen, do not make me feel so good that I cannot resist. She is a really good girl. By the way, what is the plan? Where are we going?"

"Knowing Gauri well, she would want to do something whacky. You might not know this yet, but she is a tomboy."

I heard her. I did not pay attention though. I was pulled in the ring of Gauri's thoughts. Before I could go in, Tom started walking outside with the chairs and a table. Gauri came smiling with mocktails along with cashew nuts, pringles, kebabs and pakoras. The hot and yummy gobhi, onion and mirchi pakoras stood out. It was decided that we had to live for the day.

That day I realized another thing: that friendship is crucially important. This is where I had gone completely wrong with Arya. When I was with her, it had been just the two of us. Nobody else. While I should not compare, yet I can feel the difference was vast. Here, it was all of us. More like friendships than pure passion. Precisely the reason why Tom did not like Arya during those days. And I knew I wouldn't have the liberty to think much as Gauri revealed what she was up to. She wanted to race cars. Pair up. She actually wanted to do it on a day when it had rained. She was excited about it. The race as well as the weather.

"Come on, that is what gives the kick. Muddy tracks, water, those hard turns, and that pumped up feeling."

"Wow! I feel pumped up already. In fact I feel pompeddddd up. My adrenaline is rushing. But I have never raced in my life. So all I can say to you is, you win," It was an unintended humour as I knew how serious my girl was about the whole thing.

"Hahaha! Don't concede. Dont give up without putting up a fight."

"Yeah, like I did in the game during the day."

"This is actually a man's sport. You should be gung-ho about it."

"Kinda throwing a veiled challenge?"

"Nah, it's open."

"Let us do it. Come on Tom and Itishree, don't be quiet and scared. Let us pair up."

We were on the road in no time. The way to the tracks was rather empty. It was the weekend off. We reached the point in less than stipulated time. Also governed by the fact that we were already in racing mode. It was a different story that Gauri and Itishree made it ahead of us. As expected. End of the day, it was all about the race on the muddy tracks. The race that I had to participate in, with my girl. The race that she was thrilled about. The race that seemed to take her peak of confidence high enough to take part in the rally next year. The race that I was destined to lose.

It was flagged off by the local boy. I throttled. I was doing it based on the movies I had seen. All of Hollywood was breathing inside me at that point. Tom got jerked and shaken, and was almost falling on me. He screamed a few abuses. But that was not the point. Gauri had disappeared. She had vanished. Evaporated.

Present Day

She had vanished. I told Tom. Yet again, she has vanished. Unprovoked. No ransom calls. No trace. A feeling that she was playing hide and seek would come and go. Though I did not wish to think of anything else. No way could I possibly think of any untoward incident. Hope I'd just see her spring up at my door. Sorry, I mean, at our door. Hope she'd tell me that she stretched the vanishing game a bit too far. Hope was the only hope to wait for. Seemingly fading away. Causing me uneasiness. Alas!

The tower of worry was building up. It was getting constructed with my corroborated thoughts. More so. More now. I was beginning to crumble. I did not want to. I was way too nervous. I was gaining a sense of loss. She was gone. With every hour gone by, and every moment passing away, my life was only becoming more miserable. I harbored negative emotions at that point.

The sound of the doorbell could not be heard. Not heard for fifteen minutes or so. I could hear Tom screaming from the washroom that the doorbell was ringing. I could hear Tom. I was probably not getting used to the idea anymore that someone would come to visit me. Yet again, I thought as to why was everyone going away from me.

I dragged myself to the door. It was Arya. I was shaking. So, when she shook hands with me, it was a frozen one. I was looking through her. I could not see her properly, nor could I build her image. I was talking, however it was to myself. She was finding it hard to decipher my speech. I was making no sense at all, neither to her nor to myself. I knew that, but could not control it. I was feeling hollow. The hollowness caused but a brain that had shut down. It amplified the feeling of non existence. I felt like I was dying. I felt that was the only way for me to be with Gauri. If not in life, after life is where I could live my dreams with her.

The uncertainty definitely causes more pain at times. It can even lead you to end your life, in case you cross the boundary of insanity.

"Neil, I am so sorry to hear about her. I don't think you should be left alone now."

"No, I am not alone."

"Of course, you have me."

"No, I meant Tom is here with me. So I am not alone. You hear me?"

"What about me? Now I don't feature at all in your life? I thought we had become friends."

"Of course, the circumstances and from what I have learned, you had left me all alone some time back. What brings you here?"

"I repeat, didn't we decide we shall remain friends? We have met after that. Why are you acting weird today?"

"I repeat, maybe you understand it better so let me rephrase. Today is different than all other days. Today I am not me. Today, you are not you. Today is weird...yes today is..."

"Neil, you are literally fucked up. You need me baby."

Arya came close to me. She hugged me as I looked battered. Torn apart. I was weeping. She held my hand as I was pulling myself back. My nose was running and she used her kerchief to wipe it intermittently. I was not sure what I was going through, but it almost seemed like hell. I shrugged. I threw Arya back. I had begun to shout at her. I was even mildly abusive. I reacted in a bizarre manner. I had to control before I began to despise myself and go into self pity mode. So, in a normal tone, I began to blame her for Gauri's missing case. The adapted side of mine was certainly not appreciated by Arya. However, in the given circumstances, she did not react the way she could have. Similarly, I was not aligned to this side of Arya. She again turned to me and hugged me. She kept repeating her words to me that I should vent it all out. All my anger, frustration on her. She opened her arms and kept saying sorry for all that had happened in the past. To me, she sounded genuine. To Tom, I did not know yet. My mind was simply not capable of judging anyone at this point. I believe in what I see. Tom could still try to make an inference based on his observations and maybe a better understanding of human beings than me.

Before he could be a part of this weird arrangement where two exes are trying to be nice to each other, Arya suddenly pulled out a few lines from her mouth that sent me shock waves.

"Look, Neil, I know you love Gauri. That is absolutely fine. I am here to let you know that whatever I can do in my might, I will. I shall leave no stone unturned to find your lady. I shall go to any extent to find your love. To find my friend Gauri. She had become a dear friend of mine. I feel for her and you. I shall be part of the investigations, travel if needed and any time of the day or night, I shall be at your disposal. Just give me a holler. Don't throw me out of this, just because you believe I had dumped you."

"Did you not?"

At this point, I was registering all that Arya was speaking. She sounded soothing to me. However, her last sentence kind of settled in my head, so I happily ignored all that preceded it. I only wondered what she meant when she said that she did not dump me. She very much did. I remembered that she was a loose nut.

"I did not want you to be hurt by me. I knew I was a misfit for you in this relationship. I knew I was demanding. I also knew that at no point would I be able to change myself or you. So the best was to see you happy. In love, at times, we make a decision that is not likable. However the intention is good. That is what love is, according to me. I may have chickened out, so be it. At least you are a happier soul now. Remember, I shall always love you, despite not being in a relationship with you."

"Wow, Arya! You seem to be luring my friend. Again. Don't try that on him," remarked Tom.

I knew exactly how Tom would react. But somehow, Arya was making sense to me. Friends can have divided opinions. According to me, she was correct. Had she wanted, she could have used me to the maximum. I had never left her or even wanted to leave her. It was only after Gauri had come in my life, did I begin to feel that whatever happens is for good. Whatever happens is for a reason.

"Tom, leave it. Arya is making sense. I know for a fact that she is not a gold digger. Yes, we are poles apart, and maybe she envisaged how life would be for both of us few years down the line and hence moved away from me."

"So, you wish to forgive her?"

"Well, if she means what she says, then there is no forgiveness to be granted. Also, she has gained more respect in my eyes."

Tom remained quiet. As if I was imposing the state of silence on him. It lasted unusually longer this time. I read his expressions carefully. There was a long sigh. The repartee came in from Arya this time.

She physically shook Tom and spoke out loud, "Come on dude, what is wrong with you? Tell me what have I done to you that you despise me. Did I hurt you? Did I cause you any harm? Except walking out peacefully from his life. Without any fuss or tantrums. I had a choice. I could have decided never to bother you guys. I always had the choice. I could have decided to move on, find some other guy, like Neil did. I never complained. Neil moved on within days of our break up. Did I bloody even raise my voice or show signs of madness? What does it tell you about me? Now, talk to me, Tom. Look here… look into my eyes and answer me now. I need to know from you. Do you have any answer except for that fuckin' blank expression? I can question Neil about his love for me. I can also shout and say that he was using me. He never loved me and hence it was easy for him to move on. Did I say that even once? I was the one who took a lead and asked him to remain friends. And now this is what happens to me. You are asking him to forgive me. Wow…shame on you! Why don't you just fuckin' kill me? Just because I do drugs and drink at times, you label me as someone who is not fit to be with you guys. Kill me…do you hear me…*kill me now!*"

Arya was running helter-skelter. She kept screaming and even hitting Tom without realizing. She was sobbing the next moment. Then she buried her head deep in the couch.

Tom and I consoled her turn by turn. She did elbow Tom a couple of times with full force. He could not handle her at all. In fact, we were in utter disbelief about what was happening. The situation was such. I could see Tom developing a softer side for her. Tears do draw a human being into his or her own true emotional state. The example stood right in front of my eyes.

Tom sat on the couch beside Arya. They talked at length. I left them together and went to open the door to the unforeseen guest. It was Itishree. She sounded worried. She took me to the balcony. The house was divided into two parts. My friend was with my ex and I was with my girlfriend's friend.

"I have been calling you since last evening. Where have you been?" she asked me. "Before that, I want to know what Arya is doing here," said she is a hushed tone.

"She is here to offer her help."

"Then what are the cops doing?"

"How do you know we have cops involved at this stage?"

"That's a no brainer, Neil." She looked down while she made that statement. To me, she appeared to be nervous.

I pestered her. I continued to ask her how did she make that statement so confidently. Then I asked her about her whereabouts since Gauri had gone missing. I was adamant.

"Look Itishree, you are her bestie. You know everything about Gauri. I am not doubting you, so don't get me wrong. However, I believe, you know something and you are hiding it. The cops are involved, yes. They are going to ask you tough questions too. We were in fact looking for you. They were here this morning. The case has not been registered yet. The investigation started off based on the complaint. It is therefore better you confide in me, rather than getting into any trouble with the cops. I promise to help you out. Now come out with the truth."

Itishree stood still. She kept staring madly into my eyes. I could see her clinch her fists. I was almost certain that she had something to talk about. She suddenly took a different course. The course that bewildered me more, which I was not prepared for.

"Listen, Neil. You need to tell me what had happened between you and Gauri. Was there any altercation? Gauri was slightly perturbed during the last few days. Did you notice that? You were the closest to her now. I really want to know everything, you know. Amongst all of us, you would have the maximum information. Do not forget she was living with you. Tell me everything before the cops find out something. Neil, I promise, I shall keep it a secret and try to help you as much as possible. I still believe you are good guy. Tell me the truth so I can retain my faith in you. And just because I said that the cops are involved, it gives you no right to point fingers at me, when you know that there are more fingers that can point back at you. Also remember, Gauri is my lifeline more than you could ever imagine."

"What the hell are you talking about?" I was extremely cautious and conscious now.

"Whatever you wish to understand, Neil."

"Okay, let me clear myself here since you have questioned me. Gauri and I had a beautiful life. I was always there for her. I had begun to love her. Yes, I did observe some changes in her over the last few days and I did ask her about it. But she remained mum on those topics and would try to just tell me to relax. Once she said that her exams were bothering her. The other time it was the usual girly stuff. So I found it pretty normal and then she would be okay. I did not see any reason why she would do anything. I mean, I don't want to think that she took any drastic step or ended her life. There was no apparent reason. If there was, she would have told either of us. And now, we draw a blank."

I asked Itishree to settle in the living room. Arya had gone. She and Tom discussed the matter further. I kept thinking hard. Itishree's conversation got me thinking more. I know that I was sitting on a time bomb. We could not just rely on the cops. If she were in real trouble, we needed to act. I was cursing these goddamn laws. I cursed myself further for wasting the day by being at home. I immediately called my dad. It was followed by a call to Junior Jethmalani. He gave me real valuable advice. He also asked me to trust the cops and to never be rude with them. He told me that often cops work in the background and only approach us when they need some information as they do not wish to reveal everything to avoid wrong direction or conclusion.

I began to follow my dad's advice. Like a man. It was time to inform Gauri's parents. Nobody wanted to take the risk. The college was least concerned about this. Also, considering the fact that it had happened over the weekend, simply meant that if any action could be expected, it would not be before Monday. It was not a case of any heinous crime, as it had not been proven.

"Itishree, have you informed Gauri's parents?"

"No no...no way. Auntie will die of a heart attack."

"What do you mean by that?"

"It is a straight forward thing. How can she listen to this over the phone and you expect her to remain normal?"

"Then, what is the best way you can suggest? In case this hits the media channels, then what happens?"

"It already has. It is in the afternoon daily already, Arya was correct." Tom came, confirming the shocker of the moment.

"Oh my god! It's the headline!" Itishree said, holding the couch.

Tom looked at me. I knew what he wanted to say. He was in a continued state of incredulity. He was overtly concerned for all of us. More than anything else, he was worried about Gauri's parents. He did not want to wait for any of our logic or anything. He displayed maturity and went towards the landline to make a call. I saw Itishree getting up at the sight and asking Tom to rethink about how he would break the news to Gauri's parents. She kept repeating that her mother was extremely sensitive. Well, I won't doubt her as I had experienced Gauri's sensitive side myself. So maybe she had got that from her mother. Before I could initiate anything with Tom, he was already on the phone.

"Auntie, namaste. How are you?"

"I am good, beta. Is that Neil?"

"Nahi Auntie, this is Tom. But you know Neil?"

"Arey, *humara almost neighbour hai.* I think yes it was day before that Gauri called me up and said that she is going out with Neil and her college friends over the weekend. So I should not bother her much. I know she had liked him since she was a kid and she never hides anything from me. I am so stupid. I am going on and on. *Beta aap bolo*, what makes you call me?"

"Auntie, that's what I wanted to tell you. These guys have gone and you might not be able to connect, so you need not bother. I was not feeling well, so I decided to stay back."

"That is very sweet of you. But tell me one thing, I hope this girl Iti has gone with her."

"Of course, Auntie. They are two bodies one soul," Tom said reluctantly. I could see the dreaded expression on his face. I pulled Itishree immediately. She looked completely blank. Tom joined me after he finished his conversation with great difficulty.

"Do you really think I need to ask you much? Hope you can clarify this."

"Why the fuck do you come to me? I am now in a different state altogether. You know what guys, we must try to find her on our own. These cops are useless."

"Really! Why should I not ask you anything? I still cannot believe Gauri did not tell you anything. I mean, she called up Auntie and told her about the weekend plan. I know that she wanted to spend time with me. Oh hell, she is in trouble."

I wanted to say a lot. The cops made their appearance just in time. I stopped at that. They came with some confidence. It was just Dhanya this time. She clarified that Vishwa was busy with a search with a few of his under covers.

"Listen Neil, first get me some coffee, *yaar.*"

"Oh, so you are known to Neil?" asked Itishree with a faded expression.

"Yes, yes, we are old buddies. I am helping my friend find his love and your bestie."

"Oh, so you know me too?"

"Iti, I am Dhanya, your senior at school, remember me now?"

"Damn! Blue House? Ganges Dorm?"

"Exactly."

"The world is so small. I am so happy you are part of this investigation. Now I am sure the law will help us."

"I am leading this. And we have got a few things ruled out already, so we are inching towards success. I shall speak with you later, let me speak with Neil first. Please don't mind, but could you excuse us? Thank you," Dhanya was assertive, yet polite. She gave Itishree almost a notification and Itishree disappeared into the balcony in no time.

"Dhanya, you seem to be in real control of the situation. What is the news? I am so restless."

"This is not as simple as you and I have been thinking. One thing I can assure you is that there is no hand of any professional gang, hence from that standpoint, there is no fear. We have been on it since morning. We have grilled the gym manager, the fruit vendor where Gauri bought fruits from, and everyone around the spot where Gauri was last seen. Only the gym complex has the CCTV. The roads do not have any and therefore we go clueless when it comes to any recorded evidence. Now, Gauri is seen walking out. The car parking does not have her car. I believe her car is not here too. Could you tell me where her car is?"

"We did not have parking space for two cars here. I had applied for it though. Hence, Gauri had left her car with Itishree."

"Okay, so Itishree drives the car now?"

"No, she does not know driving yet. So it must be parked right there at Iti's flat. She is not a hosteller, like us."

"Oh okay, that information helps. So at least we rule out any car jacking kind of stuff. Last year, we had a case where the robbers took the car and the owner along, killed him on the way and later on the Mumbai crime branch found that car near Indo-Nepal border," Dhanya said in a matter-of-fact manner.

"That is very scary. I believe that should not be the case."

"Do you have anything to tell me or share with me?"

"Well, since you had asked us not to step out of the house, leave alone the city, we remained confined. Arya had come over before Iti arrived. She was asking me to involve her when needed and that she was ready to provide any help or support."

"Arya is on my radar. She usually goes with Gauri to the gym, however yesterday she did not join her. That means, she would have some good reason for not doing so. Based on the gym receipt we took in the morning, she had renewed her membership. Also, a day before, Gauri and Arya went to the Swig pub, the one at Koregaon park. Were you aware of this? Now, don't tell me you did not know."

"No, I did not know that she had gone with Arya. I know that she had gone pubbing. But she did not tell me. I just saw that she was high. I wanted to talk to her the next day. But then this *kaand* happened."

"Hence, I am suspecting Arya. At the same time, I do not want to rule out anything that concerns Iti too. I suspect she knows a lot. But being a woman myself, I know it won't be as simple to extract information from these girls. Knowing that Arya is the daughter of an MLA, it will be all the more tough to crack it. Nonetheless, we are on it. And one more thing, it is out in the media already. Do not be surprised to watch it on television soon."

I was in a real confused state right now. Just like the cops were. I thanked Dhanya for all her help in this regard. I could see the feeling in her eyes. She sat there and sipped her coffee. Tom and Itishree were still in the balcony. Dhanya looked at me once again piercingly which caught my attention.

"*Neil, tu mujhse kuchh nahi hide kar raha na?* Hope this is not something else. See I am not grilling you and nor did Vishwa so far. It is because I asked him not to. But I know for a fact that he will come for you in case he finds anything. The fact that she was living with you raises many questions."

"Are you done? It was absolutely normal. Yes, like with any couple. I did not get much into Gauri's life after she told me about her exams and her monthly period that was bothering her."

"This is exactly what I want to know. Was she bothered?"

"Yes, but normally bothered."

"Are you a jerk? When a woman goes missing, there is nothing called normally bothered. Also, do I really need to tell you Neil that you should have called me up when Arya was here and whatever you found fishy. Do I need to?"

"You have to understand my state of mind. I haven't slept in the last twenty hours. You really expect me to do everything perfectly?"

"Okay, sorry yaar. But please tell me everything that you think can help us solve this case. I don't want you to lose Gauri."

I did not want to bulldoze Dhanya, nor did I want to behave erratically. I had been awake for more than fifty hours at a stretch while preparing for exams, so this was a stupid excuse. I was a twenty-year-old, with a hell lot of stamina and confidence. I had done and achieved things in life. Gauri needed me the most at this hour and it was better I behaved and did more. This was not enough. I only thanked Dhanya for giving that lecture to me. I narrated it all to her. I shared every bit of information that I possibly could, including what I observed in my conversations with Arya and Itishree.

"Exactly, this is what I wanted, hero. This is so crucial. See, I told you there is no professional hand in this. I am certain that there is something Arya and Itishree are hiding from us. Arya is into drugs. Gauri always had money due to her father's financial background. Itishree is loyal to Gauri and she also belongs to a good family. Could Arya get her kidnapped for ransom and not really triggering it as yet as the matter is hot? She had been apprehended on a couple of occasions in the past in rave parties. You'd have known this anyway. See, this is how we think. We do not spare anyone."

"I leave it to you. Please help me find Gauri. I shall give you a Europe tour package for your wedding."

"I am few years your senior. So let me tell you that I need to protect you like my junior. Okay, I have got what I needed. I shall see you soon. And do not tell anyone of what we spoke," saying that, Dhanya left hurriedly.

I waved at Tom. He got Itishree inside as well. They were curious. I did not show any signs or expressions. I was neutral. In the end, I just asked Itishree to go to her apartment as the cops would reach her anytime. She asked me what it was about. I told her it was normal routine stuff. She need not fear. Itishree insisted I tell her what it was. I avoided any further discussion. Itishree did not move. Tom found this disturbing too.

He asked Itishree what made her so nervous. She pulled her hair weirdly. Then she stepped out to the balcony. We could not comprehend what she was up to. All that we did was wait. She did not take much time. She came back in. She pulled out an envelope and handed it over to me. I asked her what it was. She remained quiet. That was an indication for us to figure out stuff now. My hands were trembling while opening the envelope.

"What is this drama, Itishree? Tell me straight what is in it?"

"This is not pleasant. I received this at my doorstep while I was coming to see you guys."

"It is more than an hour and you are telling us now?"

I opened the envelope finally as Itishree only kept beating about the bush. There was a hand written note that got us in a tizzy. It indicated that Gauri has been abducted and we must not involve the cops.

"When did you get this?"

"Today. It was pushed beneath my door."

"Why would anyone send this to you?"

"No clue."

"This has come on a Sunday. So, this is not a post."

"It is not. And it isn't a courier either."

"Someone came and pushed this under your door. Someone who knows where you stay. Someone who knows you were at home at that hour. Someone who knows you will hand it over to us and not the cops. Someone who has inside info."

"Wow, Neil, you think real smart. Yes, and now I am thinking about the intention and purpose of this letter."

"Should we not give this to Dhanya?"

"Well, I need to call her and apprise her of this, else she will put me behind bars."

I informed Dhanya and she asked me to accompany Itishree to the latter's house with that letter. I could see Itishree shivering. She lost her control completely. She started howling and burst into a pool of tears. She was nervous. She kept folding her hands and saying that we should do our best to get Gauri back. She even went to the extent of saying that she could not live without her bestie.

"Neil, you know it now and I have known it for many years that Gauri loves playing pranks, especially when it comes to troubling someone. She does it effortlessly. Hope this is all a big prank designed by her. You know, so far, I thought so. However, after receiving this letter, I am going crazy. It is like crying wolf. She is in goddamn real trouble. The whole theory of her being disturbed in the last few days seems to be ruled out after this letter."

"I am equally worried, if not more. We will act immediately. And this letter came to you after the news hit the press. That means, someone is way too smart. They are indicating that they are powerful and connected. That is all. Else this letter could have come even yesterday. Also, you know why this letter was never delivered to our apartment? Because we have CCTV cameras. Again, that means, someone is familiar with your apartment as well as mine."

We started off to reach Itishree's apartment. Tom took to the wheel. I was out on the road after a bulky twenty hours. I looked out only to feel lifeless. We reached the apartment in no time, so the negative thoughts did not prolong either. It being Sunday, there was less rush on the streets. That was the only observation I could make.

Dhanya was right there, near the parking lot. She accompanied us to Itishree's apartment. I did not want to waste any time.

"So how many people have held this envelope so far?"

"Well, me, Neil, Tom and the kidnapper."

"Hmm. Wish you had used handkerchief or gloves. Anyway, you are not trained for all this. Give it to me."

Dhanya opened it and instead of paying attention to what was written inside kept looking at the envelope and the paper. She looked at the edges as I could make out from her eye movements. She smiled. She did not reveal anything yet. She looked at me and said, "I have a clue here. Before I make my move, Iti, could you take me to the parking lot and show me where Gauri's car is parked."

"Certainly, let us go."

We could not find her car. Dhanya asked Itishree, however she feigned ignorance. She stated that she stayed late in the college and that Gauri had left early as she wanted to buy some college books and had to pay the gym fees. It was a matter of concern. We checked with the security guard and he looked at the register entry. It showed that the car was taken out at 2:45 p.m. the previous day.

The register entry suddenly struck my head too. There must be a register entry even at my apartment as I believe Gauri had come there. I remember how the room had been decorated the day she went missing. Whoops, it was only yesterday. That might throw some light on Dhanya's investigation. She agreed. At my apartment, there was no car entry. The CCTV footage was already checked by Vishwa and he informed that Gauri had been at the apartment at 2:30 p.m. The car was not seen as far as the gate, that the camera was focused on.

So, either Gauri had come to my apartment first, and then took the car from Itishree's or someone else took the car and Gauri was not aware of it. Itishree did not know driving, so there was no chance that she could have taken it out. Dhanya recorded the observations and statement and alerted us to be cautious.

The room was pitch dark. The curtains were neatly drawn closely together. It was impossible to determine the time of the day. Not a bit of light could make an entry in this gloomy paradise or hell. There was no noise either. The only thing that existed was a human body looking for a soul. The connection between the two was certainly missing. So far as the decor goes, the curtains would remind one of the old Pune families. There definitely was that Parsi touch. There were other things as well. However, the Irani chai had turned cold. It was almost frozen. The bun maska seemed okay though. But it wouldn't meet anyone's appetite. Would only go well when warm, with the hot tea. There were a couple of sedatives lying by the side. It appeared that it was a three pill strip and one had already been used. If you glanced across, though in the darkness, it was hard to notice; but if you would read the occupant's mind and body, then it was apparent that only half a tablet had been used.

Why do I not meet you soon God? I do not have much hope left from this life. Gauri kept talking in mild sleep. She seemed to be in trouble. But there was nobody else there. It was hard to make out at this point as to what was going on. It was tough to even understand Gauri's state of mind and the reason for her dilapidated condition. All that was known was that Gauri was alive and in a room all by herself. A young, happy and vivacious college girl in this state was not something anybody would believe. Therefore, the situation, a hundred kilometres away from Pune was not great. As everyone was only trying to find this girl who was living in a room that belonged to her only. This was nestled in the locale where she wanted to give Neil a surprise. She had wanted to spend time with him here. However, such was not the case anymore. One would really like to wait for her to come to her proper senses.

She had begun to move a little more. Though she had completely stopped talking, yet her movement was gaining pace, thereby suggesting that Gauri would be up from her sleep. That was an impact of the half sedative. Things would begin to get clearer in some time.

There was a movement that didn't suggest Gauri being apprehended or assaulted. She was not even forcibly drugged. She was just aloof and fighting depression from the look of it.

I don't know what's going on here. Damn! Why the heck did I sleep so much? Where is my energy gone? Too much thinking maybe. I just hope I am wrong this time. O' Gosh! It is terrible.

She kept on repeating. Her mind flickered. She reached out for the glass of water. Even in the pitch dark, she could assume absolutely perfectly where the glass was kept. She must have picked it up early on. So the room was not always like this. Of course it was a no brainer that Gauri had turned it so.

She finally decided to get up. She wiped the water off her face and some that she had spilt on her spaghetti. It was black. She wore boxers. She then started to move her hands on the bed. She was looking for her lingerie. The need to turn on the lights took a priority. She did not draw out the curtains that were still within reach and sight. She did not want to even see the world outside. It was a different thing that you could only see hill ranges. It was a soothing view. For Gauri, it did not seem to matter much. Or did it?

She twitched her eyes. Washed and splashed water on her face. Looked at the watch.

Oh God, I have two more hours to go.

She was not wearing any make up. There were no empty plates or eatable around. Only a complimentary water bottle that had been provided by the hotel.

Fariyas Resort was well located with good services. Gauri did not want to die. She always felt if she hadn't come here, she might have died. She might have consumed poison. Hanging from the fan was scary to her and falling off a tall building was never appealing. She had actually bought five strips of sedatives. It was on the way to Lonavla that she threw them all. Only a three-tab strip was what she had retained. The purpose of this was to face the aftermath.

Things could go in any direction from here, though Itishree had kept consoling her. Itishree had told her to remain calm. She had warned her about taking any drastic step. Losing in a game was acceptable to her. Losing in life was acceptable as well. Losing in love was not.

Gauri opened her diary. She was in her form. She began to write what was on her mind.

'His ravishing brown eyes, thick manly eyebrows gave me an impulse. I was in a fantasy world when I saw him in the college the first day. He had changed in the last two years ever since he had left school. I used to walk around him, go unnoticed. I used to breathe almost in his ears and find no reaction. I loved to tease him from a distance. The man who gave me seven happy years. The man who will always remain everything to me. The one whom I am madly in love with. The man whom I cannot live without, the man who gave me a reason to be here, to be away from him and testing my insecurities, means the world to me. The man who calls himself a boy.'

Seldom do I tell you what goes on in my mind...
Seldom do I tell how our distances bother me...
If only you were here to read and find...
How my soul yearns to scream 'kiss me'...
You stay away from me is not what I dread...
It's your heart distancing me what I fear...
I have no one but you and this thread...
This string of crimson roses and painful tear...
I may not be the right one for you, my darling...
But my mind and soul have surrendered my love...
My body isn't stable; it's already clinging...
For it needs nothing... but just your love...

'Neil, you have no clue how much I love you. I mean, not literally, but that's how I am thinking right now.

'Insanity. Yeah that's what hit me when I was riding rough over the past few days. I had begun to feel terribly insecure.

'To be with the man whom you have loved more than your own self is not an easy task. You have to wash away your fears. You know that is bloody hard to assuage those set of insecurities that cripple you. Come on, I am an eighteen-year-old girl. Nothing changes suddenly when you love from being 17 and 364 days to 17 and 365. You still remain a non-adult for this initial phase. I still believe I am a young girl studying in school. Fighting those eyes that stare at my boobs and butts all the time. Fighting that man's world. In my heart of hearts, I knew when I turn 18, I won't necessarily become an adult. But with my man, my handsome young dashing man, I will be more than that. More than just an adult. I know I am stupid when it comes to taking decisions. I know I will continue to be a child for some more time. Could I have stopped time? Could I have shared with you my fears? The answer is yes. Did I do it? The answer is no.

'I was not laid back. I just did not want to lose you. After all, you got me as a replacement of someone who you crazily loved and supposedly love even now. That linen in your room and that wardrobe carried her fragrance. How would I even confront you and ask you to get it out? You could not get that woman out of your life. What happened to those smells and odours that lingered on your bed for days and days.

'I came to your room secretly in the night. I kept looking at you for hours. I wanted to touch and feel you. I don't know why you never asked to touch me. I wanted to believe that it is not in you to take that lead. But Neil, I am an adult. I am your girl. Please touch me. I really want you to.

'I so much want you to drink tea from my cup, eat breakfast from my plate. Come on, goddamnit! Why would a girl take such a big step to move in with you? Why?

'Did you ever think about it? I know you love me. I want to believe you do. Do you have any freaking idea what I was going through over the last few days? I was dissolving in the universe with my world of scariest dreams. Did you know that the fear of the unknown loomed large? Did you know that I found that bottle of wine inside your closet at a place that only you and Arya had known. Then next day I find that bottle gone. Do you know that I found your old cards that you had written for Arya? I was okay with your past but it is way too much for me to face that myself. I cried a lot. I was shattered. You weren't at fault. This time you weren't. However, what led me here was the whole background to it.

'The dark lonely thoughts had gripped me. I could not stop myself from getting swayed. The horror continued to strike me. I could not talk about it. It would have gotten worse. I wasn't at peace with myself. I just hope my unfinished tasks get over now. I believe in the same.

'God cannot be that cruel as to take you away from me. It's my fight with my inner demons. When you were around, I stopped feeling that thing. In just a few days, I could feel that sense of losing you forever, and I could not afford it. You are a human being.

'You secured some of her clothes in your room. Hidden at places that I could not have seen or noticed. I did. She was asking me to locate the places.

'Every time I saw something, the smell of her began to intoxicate me. I did not want to die. That evening at the pub in Koregaon Park completely shattered me.

'Letter for you Neil:

Dearest Neil, my Neil,

My life begins with you. I am here to last forever, but not without you. I am a teenage girl holding my dreams

*together for a beautiful life with you. I am a young
simpleton who believes in no fast life except for fast
cars. I am a normal girl who believes in no lavish life
except for romantic evenings with you. I have waited for
you, and now when you are there with me, I don't want
any force in the world to stop you and me from getting
together. I won't survive then. My life begins with you
and ends with you, because for me, it's forever.*

I love you, and will always do.

*Yours (hope) lovingly
Gauri Neil Bhargava'*

The letter got soaked in her tears. The ink spread out. Gauri
blew air in a rush to not let it die out. She wasn't feeling good
about everything not going according to what she had thought.

'Mercy, my god. What have I done so wrong to you.

'Neil, forgive me for I ran away from you. Forgive me for I
wanted to test your love for me. Forgive me. I am ready to be
punished. Well, this is what I want as my reward for winning
that obfee game from you.'

Finally, Gauri planned to draw out the curtains. She
turned her phone on.

And she kept saying, 'What am I doing here. I have got to
be either here or there. Damn! I need to hold myself together.
It's nonsense crazy shit.'

She saw innumerable messages on her phone and she
knew the senders would get the delivered receipt. Yet she
opened it.

It's been twenty-three hours now. Phew! The last message
was from Itishree. It read *Please baby call me up. I am really
worried for you.*

Gauri said, 'Yes I know baby. I know you need to be spoken with. Though I am really fearing the outcome. I don't know how I am going to talk to you. Let me hold myself together.'

She spent five minutes looking out of the window. She blew hot air, this time at the window panes. Then she drew some alphabets, A and N. She did that a few times over. Then kept crossing out A. Then she drew G and A. Then she put a heart in between. She continued to thicken it and kept on murmuring to herself.

After five minutes, she turned the television on. She surfed through the channels. She was looking for herself. She smiled and turned it off. After two minutes, rang the doorbell.

Pune, around the same time

I was on the verge of collapsing. I informed Dhanya that I would be with the cops till we were able to find Gauri. She initially refused, but later agreed. She said that she needed to talk to Arya at the earliest. But before that she needed to visit the gym once and asked me to accompany her. When she said that, she meant that I could only wait outside. She was like family to me, yet she kept her profession separate. I had huge respect for her. I don't think I had any right to curse the judicial system early on. Dhanya was one example, who was part of the system and thus contributing directly. Folks like us would study, earn, pay taxes, then crib for the rest of our lives. I was happy with my decision to be with the cops. I had asked Tom to stay with Itishree and not leave her alone. My fear was that Itishree was vulnerable at this point and therefore the best was to have someone like Tom with her. She would stay strong that way.

After ten minutes, Dhanya stepped out and staggered across the side walk to the gypsy. She threw a bunch of questions at my face.

"Did Gauri have any animosity with the gym guy?"

"No way. She would have told me."

"Did Arya and Gauri come to the gym together regularly?"

"Yes, they were gym partners and worked out together, as far as I know."

"Where can we find Arya at this hour?"

"If you want, I can call her right away."

"Yes, please do. I doubt if she would talk to you now. She knows we are looking for her."

"She herself appeared at my place and offered help."

"Precisely the reason why you are in trouble today."

"What do you mean?"

"You are so naive, Neil."

I kept quiet. I could sense that Dhanya was suspecting Arya of some foul play, however it was hard for me to understand anything at this stage.

"Her number is not reachable. I believe there is some network issue or her battery died out."

"Okay. Take me to her house then."

In ten minutes, we reached her house. I got a call from my dad. He wanted to inform me about the meeting with the lawyer. I told him to call me back in some time. Then he said something which did not allow me to hang up. The news of Gauri was already widespread. Her parents had got to know about it and they were in touch with my parents. He told me that Gauri's number was not reachable. After an exchange of few points, I comforted them. Then I checked my message to Gauri and it showed delivered. I jumped and screamed. Thankfully, Dhanya was around. She dialled Gauri's number, but it was turned off. She called up Vishwa and asked him if there was any way to find based on the number, the whereabouts. Vishwa apparently told her that he would try his best. In their unit, technology was still a challenge.

Dhanya and I talked about the events. She mentioned that chances were that the kidnappers must have thought of using the phone and turned it on. Later they must have taken the SIM out and thrown it. That was one theory. There were several others that were being discussed. She told me to join her for the meeting with Arya as she did not want any political influence to play any role in the investigation. The reason why Dhanya was in civil dress was also because she wanted the interrogation process to go smoothly.

She rang the doorbell. Arya opened it in no time as if she knew we would turn up.

"So, Neil, you decided to come with her or she asked you to come? Well, if it is about interrogation, then I hope you know me well."

"How can I ever forget you, Arya? This time, you seem to have made a big mistake," Dhanya said confidently.

"If you are calling me a convict, I can call up someone who will call you up right now and then you will have to leave the house. The reason I won't do that is because you have come with Neil. Apparently, you happen to be close to Neil. This young boy and I have had a lovely relationship. I love him and I can tell you, he does too..." Arya went on.

Dhanya stopped her in between, "Look Arya, you started it. I never came to you for an interrogation. And this is not about you being caught with drugs."

Arya tried to overpower Dhanya with her harsh tone and attitude. Never in my life had I seen anyone speak like this with a cop. I was not sure why Dhanya was being normal.

"Dhanya ji, I want to share a story with you," Arya said. "Many years ago, there lived a king named A. I am abbreviating it so that you enjoy the story and not get into the medieval history. A was an extremely powerful human being in the region. He was a brave and gallant soldier too. He never feared anyone. He had four wives. I mean the queens. He loved them equally. He would try his best to spend equal time with all. He was loved by his kingdom. He would forego the farmer's loans. God was also extremely pleased with the king, so he never had to face any natural calamities in his region. The lands were also mined with ores. The mineral output was class apart. There were diamonds and gold in plenty. The crops were world class. The kings of other regions were overtly jealous of him. They united against him and thought of capturing his kingdom and then later dividing it amongst them. That way, they would partake the richness the region offered. They came all prepared for the war. King A was not prepared for any war as he had never harmed anyone. So he was living a normal life. Then one fine day, his army announced that they had been attacked by the neighboring kings from far off regions. The king apparently did not have many troops. He simply surrendered to God. Within no time, there was the return of the enemies. God sent his angels. They made the announcements to the attacking armies through their angels and messengers. The announcement stated that while all the army of the fellow kings had reached here to captivate this good soul's kingdom, his army has marched towards their kingdoms in bulk and hence they would lose all their treasures and queens and lands that they had. Further, it would rain so heavily with storms that the entire troops would be washed off. The rivers would overflow. The eagles would feed off their flesh for they were loyal to the king and his people. Fearing such severe consequences, they decided to recede in humiliation and guilt.

"Considering you are an intelligent woman, hope you understand the moral of the story. When you are a good soul, there is a protector up there who shall save you from all the torment of the enemies."

"Excellent story, Miss Arya. We are in *Kalyuga* now. Anyway, I will only ask you a few questions. We will keep it simple."

"Ask, for I am always there for Neil."

"Why did you really feel the need of sending that letter about Gauri's abduction yourself? If you had involved professionals, they could have done it themselves."

"What is the proof?"

"Look at this letter you sent. Look at the corner carefully. It is yellowed. I had gone to the gym to talk to the manager. We found a similar letter head bundle over there. Apparently that was kept at the manager's desk. You tore a piece and played this silly game. What else can I expect from a nineteen-year-old kid who is apparently doped?"

"What rubbish? I have no fuckin' clue what you are talking about. Why don't you talk to the manager about it and I am not sniffing... this ain't dope.... you...."

"I have got everything in place, Arya. Your game is over," Dhanya lambasted her.

Before Dhanya could continue, she received a call that got her to move out of the place in a jiffy. While she ran her way out, she told Arya, "Just do not leave the city. And by the way, keep your phone on and charged."

Vishwa had called Dhanya. He had some vital information. His team had found some leads after investigating the CCTV footage that sent my spine chilling.

"It is hard to believe. Why would she do something like this?"

"I don't know Neil. Let us get this sorted one at a time. This is not what we are thinking. This seems to be something else. I don't think it will be that easy to solve."

"Don't say that Dhanya. If you lose hope, what will happen to me?"

"See, it is very easy for me to pull up Itishree based on what Vishwa has revealed. I can use stern words, but then I don't want to do that. I don't want to use force. Considering the fact that Gauri might be in real trouble, I do not wish her to be endangered any further."

Fariyas Resort, Lonavala

The letters continued. She was beginning to write a new one. Apparently, this was not written in her diary. It was on an A4 size paper. She seemed to have been prepared to write.

'Dearest Neil, my Neil,

I am here. Back again. I just moved away from your picture for ten minutes. It seemed my life has turned topsy turvy. What a beautiful picture of you it is. I can't get enough of you. Please do not ever leave me. Please do not ever leave me for Arya. Whatever you and she had, if you come and tell me about it, I shall forgive you. I will not ask you. I want you to tell me on your own. I don't want your body to smell of hers. I don't want your lips to hide her name. I don't want your heart to ever remember that there was anyone else who had ever lived there. I know I am being way too selfish right now, but that is how it is. I don't know if coming here was the right decision, however I got led into it. I got sucked

*in the situation. I could not control my mind. I could not
control my heart. I could not.....'*

Gauri broke down completely. She was undeniably devastated.
It seemed that she was not in her complete senses. Something
had mysteriously overpowered her. Something that she could
not understand herself. It was rather inexplicable.

*'Neil, I need you my handsome boy. Don't ever leave me.
Hope you are happy, now that I've called you a boy.'*

While she was lying on the bed, she began to think and
write about the moments spent with Neil and otherwise over
the last few days. Well, those otherwise moments were crucial
to her life situation today.

❖

How it had begun seven days ago

It was a breezy morning. The rains had stopped two days ago.
The air carried some chill from the past effect. The sun had been
playing hide and seek too. The mood remained brightened. Neil
had dropped me to the college and was on his way to Planet
M. He was supposed to buy me some music and a few movies.
I had given my list of Zeppelin, Van Halen, AC DC albums. He
was surprised at first. A girl who is more into Casablanca and
Bryan Adams and Phil Collins was now shifting to heavy metal.
I told him I was an adult now. Hence, I would do it all. I would
go heavy in life. I had turned heavy, weight-wise too. I had a
few pimples on my face. My skin was breaking. I did not have
stretch marks. This was the first time my skin was fattening.
So it would come later when I shed off. I really wanted to shed
it off. I was not happy about it. Apparently, music, movies and

my man – these M's were making my life. At no point so far, the pimples or fat seemed to bother me so much. Little bit only. Like any teenager.

So what made me switch to heavy metal was not just my desire or curiosity to shift overnight based on my adulthood. It was also the peer pressure. Plus the college girl thing. That pressure to be recognized. I was a girl from Guwahati in Assam. I was now in Pune. This is the modern hub. So I needed to adjust a bit. I also needed to keep on impressing my man with my style and persona that was driven by art and culture and that panache. The latter does not come with mere education or background. It has an equal contribution by the societal stuff. So there was I. Vulnerable. Enterprising. An explorer.

Arya met me in the day time. What happened after that shall be shared in a while. As I write, I shall begin to address you directly now, Neil. To the best extent possible.

That evening was the most fun evening. I got drawn into the adventure. Unrealistically. No realization as to how. It was pure and absolute delight. Maybe not pure, maybe not sane. Everything that is sane does not kick you enough to feel alive. Sanity is fine for the four walls. But when you are out, you get drawn towards what is not so sane. Like my fast cars. Like my fun games. It was a level above that. I was delightfully happy with you, Neil. I just got that extra kick. Thanks to your ex-girlfriend. She and I have done quite a few joints of cannabis by now. When I say quite a few, I mean literally. Like almost every day. In your absence, through the night and some part of the day. In your presence, I sneaked into the gym restroom. Trust me, it was more kicking than forecasting weather or watching movies. I was on a high. Elevated. Blue.

When Itishree used to tell me those stories of Manala cream, I would only wonder why people would do it. Slowly I had begun to wonder why people wouldn't do it. So the damage did not happen overnight. In fact, it never began from a sob story. It only began from happiness. The pleasure of having a boy in your life who you madly, crazily, deeply love, gives you freedom to explore life. Well, it did strike me a hell number of times to tell you. It did. I swear on my mom, Neil. But then you and Arya had broken up because she was an adventurous soul. I did not want to lose you. So the damage was not done overnight. It did not take many days either. Just that long night. One night and I was all set. Actually, in a way, it was overnight only, this seems to be the effect of that sedative. Thankfully, there was no addiction to it. But yes, I was addicted to happiness. I was damaged as I wanted to be happier.

When Arya told me that evening how you would smell her underwear every night, I ignored your fetish. Deep dark secrets of lovers should never be revealed. But when you are doing hashish together, you want to know and talk about only those dirty secrets. I used to enjoy those talks. She even showed me your pictures fucking her in the car. You did on the front seat, back seat, out of the car, and even on the bonnet. By the way, those were classy shots. I tried asking her who was taking those pictures. She smiled. She could have simply said it was the timer, but she did not say so. She smiled. Then she laughed till we moved to our vodka. I love the fact that Arya was having vodka with sugarcane juice. I had never seen or heard of anything like that in my entire life before. So I tried it too. I puked. She cleaned it up. We were at her place after spending that night in the pub. Everyone knew about you both in that pub, Neil.

That man knew you both. Then most of the smartly dressed boys were aware about your hangouts. I was taken aback. No, I did nothing to figure that out. It kept happening on its own. I don't remember how exactly, but my assumption states that it started with my dress. So this man while taking the drinks order, remembered that you had gifted a similar dress to Arya. Well, Neil, I think I was wearing the same dress, that you had apparently gifted me. Remember the one with a deeper back cut that was deep purple in colour.

What a bloody coincidence! Arya did not say anything. Imagine, this manager remembered it. So it was special. You had booked this place for some occasion. So when he showed his surprise, I kinda looked at Arya weirdly

Isn't this strange for a manager to remember your dress? I mean, who does that? Why would you be so free and open with the restaurant manager. Of all the people, this.... I rejected the whole idea and bashed that man in her absence. I wanted to say much more, but then Arya took the conversation forward.

"There is a story behind it, my dear darling. This manager was standing right across when the wine spilt on it. I made a scene."

"Oh, that's how it is remembered."

"Yeah, that's apart from the fact that he and I have been here quite a few times," Arya said assertively.

I remember how I kept thinking. I had a choice – to leave or to get grooved in. If I had left, I would have sulked and brooded. I stayed back because I knew I would sink in the pleasures to come my way.

"So, Arya, Neil gave me the same dress that you had left behind at his place."

"I won't say much. Let's change the topic. I am here to make you happy."

That moment onwards, she began to come closer and became my good friend after that puking episode. Drinks got us close, hangovers got us closer and then the Manala cream got us the closest. Obviously stated.

That's how it had all begun. I was sinking in happily. All the way in.

Arya was a rich spoilt girl. I was rich and not spoilt. I mean, not spoilt by the richness. For anything that could spoil me otherwise had not become my addiction yet.

By the end of that evening, I had received seven text messages from you. I looked at them like pearls of love. I wanted to ask you about the dress, but I stopped. Like as many as seven times. With each text that prodded me, my inner self was powerfully dominating to stop me. Also, I did not want to spoil my brilliantly shining mood. I am not a person to screw up things all the time or anytime. I have patience. I would have asked you later but then something else happened that just did not let me talk about it. In fact, many things happened later.

"Awesome yaar, you look super sexy in these hot pants and bra. Can I kiss you?"

"In the hostel you will find quite a few lesbos, Arya. By the way, you can kiss me."

Arya kissed me on my lips and I pushed her back.

"Are you fuckin' kidding me? You are desperate for love. You need a guy."

"I had yours for long. Now I need his..."

For once I thought she was high, but when she burst into hysterical laughter, I was clear that she wasn't serious.

"Meri kiss toh phir tune muft main le lee."

"Ab tu mujhse pyar ke paise maangegi?"

The flow did not halt. The spirits did not either. What had stopped were my texts to you.

The conversation with Arya was not as easy the other night. When she met me in the afternoon, I was first taken aback. Not with the meeting, but with the evening proposal. I had far too many questions. Then, I figured that she was already back in talking terms with you. I wanted to yell at you like a small town possessive crazy nasty girl who can lose her mind when she finds something amiss in the whole scenario. I transformed the entire set of my volcanic feelings into an ice chilled wave and smile. You simply smiled back. You were kinda trying to indicate to me that it was absolutely fine to talk to Arya and you got no issues with it, whereas, fucker, I wanted you to join me in our conversation as I was simply not comfortable. The only thing that pushed me forward was my art of hiding insecurities. Like I have been doing for the last seven years.

She had hugged me tight. That's when her smell caught on to me. As we progressed through round one of talks, I found her smooth.

"Gauri, I want you to know that if ever you need anything, you have your alter ego here. I know it is Itishree and I don't want to take her place, but then, don't ever think you mean any less to me."

"These words were rare to be heard in today's time and age. I love rarity. That's why I found you as my companion the most worthy of them all. He was the best rare man around. I just hope you turn out to be a good human at the end of it all."

"Arya, I don't know what it is about, but I feel that connection with you."

"Yeah, say that one more time. I simply crave for friendships. You know, Gauri, I do not get along with many people out here. Most of my friends are boys as they are harmless. Girls envy me. I really don't know why, but they do. Sounds weird that I shall become fond of my ex's girlfriend. I am weird anyway."

It was just the two of us. I had kept this away from Itishree. And can you beat that? I kept it away from her. Even Arya called her my alter ego. But I hid it all. Well, at that point, it did not sound so complicated. I do have some guilt now...at this point when I am writing it all down. I felt I was guilty of hiding my emotions.

"I am weird too. I find you smooth and easy to get along with. I hope you give me some tips about Neil. Haha just kidding."

Arya came close to me, silently said in my ears, "Tonight."

She remained in my ears for long enough to make me feel inquisitive.

"What's there tonight?"

"It will be memorable. You shall discover your man a lot more than you would do the whole of the year."

"That sounds super exciting."

"Because you shall know more about him or you will get to spend time with me?"

I simply laughed it off. So when the dress incident happened in the evening, it was not part of the planned discovery rather a mere bad coincident that was still left for clarification, an option I would or would not exercise.

I could not meet you the entire day. Just that wave from you in the afternoon. You were busy with your college stuff and I was busy with my hip hop life. Not really to that extent, but certainly no less either.

Arya tried to compensate for a lot of things. She didn't need to, but then, I could sense that she was trying to make up for your absence for the coming two days. That was her love. I could see that. She got me a lovely pack of L'Occitane cream for my face. I knew it was not available in India. I was overwhelmed with her gesture. She presented it to me just before we were to leave the pub for her place. That made us spend a good time just outside her car. We talked and talked. We laughed too. We were slightly high. I held her hand and asked her if I could kiss her. She immediately replied, "As many as you want honey. I won't charge you for it."

I kissed her palms. Like I wanted to thank her for coming in my life. She pressed her cheeks on my lips. I gave her a peck. She hugged me and said something that I can never forget. Something that moved me. Something that had tears rolling down my cheeks. An emotional aftermath of a few drinks showed up like this.

"May god give you all the strength and positivity and all of it that is there in the universe."

"Why do you like me so much, Arya? You continue to do something or the other for me. You are so nice to me, in return I have not done anything for you."

"Because you are the only girl, I sensed, who does not want anything from me. You are the only girl who is not jealous or in competition with me. Last but not the least, and this is the big reason, you loved Neil for so many years, yet when you had come here, you did not say or do anything. I had observed you a few times how you would keep crossing Neil, but that was it. That kinda impressed me helluva lot, baby. Need to know more?"

"OMG! Really. I can't believe there is so much that goes in a girl's mind while making a decision. I do not think too much. I just go with the flow."

"I would not have said all this to you normally. *Thoda high hu na*...hence said the truth."

We got into our ride and reached her place in no time. Arya suggested I call Itishree too, but I refused. I had told her that I would be with Arya today and maybe in her presence she might not open up. Itishree was fine with it.

I retired to the couch in her living room. She did not let me sleep and told me how she would introduce me to more happiness. She wanted me to participate in the entire exercise of rolling a joint. She had given a hundred rupee bill to me, exactly what she had also retained. Trust me, the excitement of rolling a joint was far more than getting admission into college.

"This is fun, ain't it? This is what craziness is all about. When we have a large gathering, then we shall go for the blunt. A joint is good for us both."

In the background, we had Aerosmith doing the magic for us. I was swaying and swirling. Rolling a joint wasn't too tough for someone like me, who shifted gears at a high speed and maneuvered like nobody else and could vanish at the snap of a finger. Arya looked startled. She could not believe at first.

"*Tu toh meri bhee guru niklee yaar.* Fuck, you have rolled two and I got just one done."

"Now don't tell me I've to teach you how to inhale it. I guess I have seen those boys in Hollywood. *Guwahati main bhee TV aata hai and ye sab chalta hai.*"

"Commendable."

In a well-paced time, we reached the roach. I did not want to go blue and go crazy. Nor did Arya. We were in a lifted mood.

"So what do you want to know about Neil?"

"Honestly, everything that is worthwhile about the most handsome dashing man on the planet."

"You are one of a kind, Gauri. You waited seven years long to get him. God also favoured you when we broke up."

"Arya, tell me na...honestly...why did you dump him?"

"Yeah, after these puffs you surely are going to ask me everything. Make me more uncomfortable na," Arya began to tickle me. What she said next froze my blood.

"He isn't what he appears to be. He is a closet lover. He will not acknowledge you in public. He will be the best in private."

"That's all fine but what do you mean by a closet lover?"

"He appears to be a one woman kind of guy, but in reality he is not. He used to have chics at home even when he was dating me. Not necessarily at his home, it could be friends' or even the hotels nearby."

"I don't believe it, Arya. What are you talking about?" I got up immediately and walked across the room steadily. In fact, I was floating now. I knew I was slurring and not well coordinated, but my sense to understand was intact so far.

Your face is morning dew,
Thickening like dough
Like memories do between gasping days
Aberrant movements, hesitant flesh
You face is a white dream. A burning sky.
Damp, feverish mountains
I inhabit its lucidity,
Its tensile dreams, its flickering warmth
Thickening kindness of sloping cheeks
That crinkle beyond sunset

I dwell on your scent.
Your scent that has demolished all sense
That covers my body,
Swishing blades of plush green
I am volatile.
Existing in isolated minutes.
Distances in my belly.
Fountains. Spurts. Cries.
Crooked elbows damaging the sky.
Wandering in abrupt desires. Outspoken desires.
Voracious red dreams. Arms, body, horizon.
My body, a sticky pink mass.
Condensed in fear and levitating in joy.

My upward tilted chin,
Swivelling
Swallowing your breath
Holding it hostage
In flesh, in body, in organ
Until the idea of you is more profound than life.

I was feeling joyfully vacant now. The kick had set in. I returned to the couch as I just wanted to remain calm. So instead of going mad, I was cool and kept on instigating Arya. She was lying on the floor.

"He is a Casanova. If I tell you he is still interested in me, then do not be surprised. In your absence, he still calls me at home and has sex with me. I am sorry for cheating on you, but often I feel he might ruin my future if I don't give in to his needs. I had dumped him precisely for the reason. But Gauri, with you, I have that confidence that you will get him on track. Though he does not talk about you at all when we meet."

"What else? Why do you think I would want to be with him even for a second? Why? There is no way I shall compromise when it comes to adultery. It's been only a few days with him and I thought I've found my heaven. I really wish to call him right now and fuck his happiness."

"No, don't do that. Never act in rage. Never react when you are high. He is anyway not here tomorrow. Plan when you are least emotional."

I was not in the right frame anyway. I kept asking Arya to tell me more. I kept becoming emotional. I was blabbering. She said a few more things that I wasn't able to comprehend. By now I was also on the floor with my legs on her. She and I kept talking, God knows what. We even giggled. Anything after that was not stored in my memory. What a weirdly horrifying night it was!

Neil, if you were anywhere near me, I might have killed you brutally that night. And I might have done that happily. Like a vampire, I would have sucked your warm blood.

You were a closet lover. Bloody, this discovery has fucked my mood, Neil. I have been living in with you and now I understand why you rarely felt my skin even when I was so close to you. Arya and maybe more were satisfying your needs. Fuck man!

The wait for the next day was not long, except for those minutes when I was engulfed in the smoke and curls of puffs. I was singing mildly, and honestly, it gelled well with Tyler's performance of that 'Crazy' song. I don't know how many times I sang songs in a male voice.

And then the dance steps were mostly tribal. I vaguely remember how I fell down after my legs were entangled during my dance steps that did not go quite well. Arya and I even used screw drivers to separate my legs. Later on she applied oil to smoothen them. That was the effect of our Manala cream night.

Sleep caught on thereafter. I woke up to wounds on my legs, not because I had fallen down, but the extreme impact of using the tip of the screw driver. I doubt if I ever fell down. My back and bums were in perfect shape.

Arya woke up instantly and we were smelling lemon grass.

"Fuck! My head is heavy. *Tune kuchh joint main milaya thha kya?* I feel you mixed it with something," laughed Arya.

"Haven't you noticed these scratches on my legs?"

"Only if you'd notice, this joint is shoved in my pussy."

"Hahahahahahahahaha! I forgot my pain, Arya. We must have been up to something. I only have faint memories. But I remember everything you told me about Neil. Wish it were a bad dream."

"Gauri, please treat it like a bad dream. I am sorry I should not have spoken anything about him at all."

"Will you just shut up? I would have disowned you if you hadn't told me the truth. You are such a selfless girl. Itishree would be happy to meet you."

I waited for the next day to unravel more. These deep dark secrets needed a place to reside. My heart held them. Bitterly. Caged. Reserved.

The coffee got me some freshness. If I had to sum up my night that I had spent with Arya, I suppose it gets a 12/10. A perfect score. Would have been 10 with Arya, additional 2 for the cause of the wounds.

So I kept on insisting. I behaved like a child. She confirmed she would tell me a lot more after joining the gym with me. I was super excited on hearing both the things. I was in awe of this girl.

Neil, you did not text me. I did not text you either. I don't know why you did not text me...maybe you knew I was with Arya. Though I wondered why you were not troubled by the fact that I was with Arya, who was your ex. And I, your present, was bloody spending time with her.

Arya kind of read my mind as she saw me flirting with my phone.

"He is like that only. He was least adventurous when it came to stuff like this. He is least responsive. He gives more space than you need. And the only reason why he would do this is because he finds his love in the space that he wants and desires or maybe with another girl. Okay, Gauri, roll this one fast, I need it. Thanks baby for helping me with the gym. I needed that badly. Now we will go together. Yay yay."

"Shut up! This is nothing I have done. Do you want me to heat up the ham or it will go fine like this? And Jacob Creeks or this Merlot thing?"

"Pour me Jacobs. Okay, look up in the shelves that is right to the microwave. See those cool French glasses for wine."

I gave what I was smoking to her. I simply did not realize what I was slipping into. Like I said earlier, I was happily sinking. Itishree was supposed to join us later in the evening today. She had her cousin over, forgetting her name. Mehr, I suppose. She would drop her to the airport and join us when she returned. This would be the second time I would be sinking in something without her. This adventure was new to me too.

"So, he is sleeping with you, right? "

"Yes, and I come to your apartment in your absence often. I said that to you yesterday and I repeat it. I do visit."

"When you go to your apartment and Neil is back, you have an option to confront him or I give the evidence to you so you can show with proof or whatever choice you have, I leave it to you. I still believe he needs some direction and you can correct him. You might need to approach it delicately."

"Is it the weed effect that I feel like killing him every time I suck this up? Or it's the fact that he is fucking around and I am finding that hard to digest ? Or is it something else? I need you, Arya. Tell me please. Shall I call him right now and clear the air? But tell me something...why are you telling me all this? Tell me Arya, why are you telling me all this?"

"Okay fuck it and fuck it all. Listen to me now. Neil told me that he still loves me. Now baby, pay attention to each and every word I say."

"Tell me Arya. Just tell me. Everything now. Don't wait for tomorrow. I need to know it all, right now. Now as in now."

"Neil told me that he still loves me. I asked him about everything that happened in the past. I asked him why did he cheat on me? Why did he move in with you? He told me that he is not much into you anyway. He is not physical with you and that in the past he never cheated on me. I knew he was lying, but I don't know how I could not control myself when he kissed my ears. I gave myself away. Then I saw him behaving normally with you the next day so I felt weird and wanted all of it to stop. But I slept with him again. After that when I saw the innocent you, I determined there was something drastically wrong about all of this. That's all. I just felt I was being physically used, and before it gets too late, I want you to control him. I don't like him to be in any kind of relationship with me. It's over. But I feel you have a chance."

"I got it. I don't want to confront him. He will come up with several reasons and excuses that I won't ever know the truth. Yes, I feel like killing him because I am too much in love with him. After killing him, I will finish myself. What's the point of living such a life?"

Arya was quiet. She kept looking down at the floor.

She did not move her head up at all. I kept on observing her. I could not figure what was happening to her. Then she held my hand and asked, "What are you thinking?"

"I got scared at first. You had stopped talking. No, there is no point thinking normally right now. It ain't that easy. If I tell Neil he will lie and I will lose him forever. What is the guarantee that he won't approach you after I sort it out? How do I figure out if he really loves me? I mean, there is nothing left to figure really. Oh gosh! I am so confused. Can he leave you?"

Arya remained quiet. I was getting high. At that point, it seemed that even Arya did not know what she wanted. I was clear though at many points that I wanted you in my life like the way I had loved you. The only thing that made me reluctant in facing you with these questions was that if there was any falsity in it, you would leave me. I had to tread things with caution. Arya told me that she shall try to prove it in her own ways. I bought her point.

The answers remained unresolved as we were joined by Itishree. She blasted me for doping. She literally argued with me. Then she was calmed by Arya.

"It's okay. Also, she is not in a great mood. *Kabhi kabhi chalta hai, tu bhee le.*"

"If I do, then who will handle her. By the way, what happened to her mood? Till yesterday it was all fine."

Arya immediately took charge of the conversation.

"Let me tell you. Because Gauri has been completely exhausted knowing some of the bitter truths about Neil. He is two-timing her. She lives in with him but he calls me over in her absence."

"What the fuck are you saying? This is unbelievable. I know him. He can never do it. Gauri loves him like mad. Well, if that is true, then that makes Neil a prick. But how do we trust you? Anyway, I am sure you must have discussed it with Gauri."

"Tomorrow, when you go home, check in the inner shelf of Neil's almirah. There is a similar wine bottle. Day after next, you won't find it there as we have plans to finish it together."

"What the fuck yaar! Arrey that's why I was wondering why would he make you a friend after you had broken up and that too so soon, when Gauri just came into his life. *Thoda toh time deta na.*"

"Iti, I cannot live without him," said I.

"But can you live with him after knowing all this?"

"I don't know, but I can't lose him."

"Let's think of how we should take it forward. The idea is that you should not lose him. He should forget Arya. And you remain happily ever after. It's all fuckin' messed up yaar."

"That's what love is. No love story is as simple. I'm shattered and still smiling because somewhere I have that belief that it's all going to be fine. But when I know each time he is still close to Arya, I feel like killing him. And I know that if I confront him, I will lay bare. I will say it all. Make it messy. Then leave him. But if I don't confront him and think of something smarter? Oh gosh! I feel like dying."

"Shut up! Never say that."

"Agree, don't think of dying. You are a brave girl."

That evening, Itishree and I left for her place. I had carried some dope with me.

"Iti, look I have a certain idea."

"Arya, before we leave, what is your final word?"

"Listen girls, I know one thing for sure. Just like Neil is away for these two days, if Gauri goes out even for a day, there are chances that he might try to come back to me permanently. It is always my choice to accept him or not. I am a human too. We know he is a closet lover, but as girls, and I don't know why god has made us like this, we are kind of forgiving and try to always think of building a relationship more than breaking it. I am not saying that it will happen in this case, but the only test for Neil would remain when Gauri is out of his sight."

We both just listened to Arya with utmost care. None of us reacted. It was not needed. We had spoken enough, heard enough. We finally headed back to Iti's, I mean my earlier sweet home.

The moment I entered, I got charged with some energy. I was high and happy. There was a freaking change. I immediately pounced on Itishree. I know I was upset from within, but then, in her presence I strangely felt better.

She did not talk to me. She kept telling me that I got screwed in the twenty-four hours of my time with Arya.

"Think about it, Gauri. Why does she smoke weed? Why doesn't anyone talk to her in college? Are you getting my point? Why on earth are you being influenced by that bitch?"

"Not even once did she say anything that would influence me. She was neutral. I only insisted that she tells me more. She wants me to settle down with him. She candidly admitted. So that way, she hasn't been wrong yaar."

I don't know what happened to me, but I could not resist pulling out another joint. I could not stop thinking about Neil. I still love him. Despite all that I have heard.

"Iti, I remember one thing that Arya had said. She had told me that if I leave Neil even for a day all by himself, he will go back to Arya. But I don't want to believe it."

I inhaled heavily to the point of turning blue. I was on the verge of making a life-defining decision. I wanted to run away for a day from everyone. I wanted to know if you would go back to Arya. I wanted to know if I was imposing myself on you. I wanted to know if my love was a mere liability. I wanted to know if you were a closet lover. I wanted to know it all.

"I will return in twenty-four hours so that the cops don't file an FIR and my headache lessens. You don't worry about mom. I will tell her I am going out with Neil and my college friends for a trip."

What was going on in my head was nothing short of a revolutionary thought. Only as an eighteen-year-old could I think of something like that. Whatever short I would have been, was duly compensated by the weed.

Itishree was taken aback by the proposal. I offered her the dope, but she refused. Her logic remained the same, as to who would then handle me.

Present Day

Arya

Umm, I can never forgive you, Neil. You asshole. Who the fuck do you think you are? I moved out of your life for just a few days and you moved on. You moron, you bastard. And Gauri, you mother fuckin' horny bitch. You found nobody else? You only had to take my man. I spent every moment of my six months with him. I can't get over his smell. I cried every single night without him. That day, I wanted to say sorry to him and get him back in my life. But Gauri, you spoilt my whole plan. You spoilt my life indeed. I so much wanted to kill you that night. But then I knew that won't be right as I would lose all my chances to get Neil back. I wanted to draw you towards committing suicide.

But that bitch Itishree came in. She came in like your saviour. She is a horrible loser. Hope she dies soon.

If I can't have Neil, you can't have him either. If I can't live, you can't live either. I hope and believe you actually never return, Gauri. Wherever you are, I just hope you have finished yourself.

I tried to sneak into Neil's house in his absence. Like a freaking desperate woman to rub myself on his clothes. Like a bitch trying to feel you in those clothes. And then leave my fragrance on. So I could tease you. So I could make you feel like a loser. See you cry in front of my eyes. See you scream. To let you talk of killing Neil. I enjoyed every bit of it.

That dress never came to the pub. It was never donned by me. It was never a gift from Neil. You are so naive. You trust people. You are a typical small town girl. Stupid. Grown up on old movies and considering yourself a star. That's what makes you vulnerable. I knew that's what you are. It was easy for me to get you hooked on to weed. Quite easy. No force. No blackmail. No emotional stuff. Just talked about you and your man and you were in. Well, yes, as a friend I took your innocence away. You were quite innocent. Ignorant.

The reason why you never had the guts to call up Neil. You knew if you had called him, and spewed your venom, you would have lost him forever. But the chances were I would have lost him too. So yeah, that was all fine.

Even when I'm writing this now, I so much want to fuck you hard, Neil. Fuck your friend, Tom. I came to your place several times. And then Tom never left your sight. I had to lie through my teeth. I lie all the time. What have you made of me, Neil? I was never like this. I was always a loyal, honest, trustworthy woman, just for your love.

You were my man. I was hovering around you like a bee all the time. I wanted to try all the possible adventures with you. Your eyes turned me on. Your whispers in my ears turned me wet. Your touch gave me orgasms. I have felt my breasts thinking of you. I have rubbed my tits imagining you. I have not stepped out of my shower because I felt you were with me rubbing soap on me and hence wanted me to stay longer. I even closed my eyes only to realize you now stay in my thoughts.

It took you no time to move on. It took you no time to get hooked up with this dumb girl who fuckin doesn't know what high class life is.

Think about it Neil. Think about it when you are fine to think.

Now that you have thought about it and you still find yourself confused, look around yourself. Is Gauri around you? No, right? Am I around you? No, right?

Do you realize that you are responsible for it? You are responsible for the situation that Gauri is in today. You had lost me earlier because you were literally willing to be detached from me like I was imposing and then...that...b.i.t.c.h!

Arghhhhhh.I curse you Neil!

What will you gain? You told that cop... that fuckin' bitch Dhanya that I am involved in it. Do what you can do. *Saala mera baap uska transfer kara dega!*

You lousy son of a bitch Neil.Had I wanted I would have got Dhanya transferred right away. How dare she question me? She had no right to do so, but you know, still I remained quiet for you. I don't know what bloody karma I have done to be in this situation today. Every time I came to your house Neil, I wanted to piss on the bed that Gauri sleeps in. What a great show off for the world to see that you sleep in two separate beds.

I scream in the universe so loud as to have hell here for you Gauri, where you rot forever. May the pain engulf you so badly that you forget what living a life is all about. I want misery for you. Plain death won't satisfy me.

And you Itishree, I repeat it, you shall die every day till you live. You will cry and regret being that alter ego.

She had turned completely pale and cold. She had consumed sleeping pills and inhaled a couple of joints as she had lost her sanity.

After crying out loud, she went to pick a knife and floated into her bath tub. She dipped herself till neck deep and began to write Neil in water. The ink came from the wounds she had begun to inflict on her body. She kept smoking the weed. Within a few minutes, she fainted.

❖

Neil is completely innocent. Call asap. Your phone is not reachable.

That text was not just a text. It was everything that said that whatever had happened over the last twenty-four hours should not have happened. It was everything that cleared it all about the goodness of people.

That message just shook Gauri and literally got her out of the grave. She was scattered like a piece of dead fish on the bed. She was running a high fever. She punched her face. She was not able to move quite well. She called up Itishree immediately.

"Damn! Gauri, the whole world has turned upside down over here. Why the heck did you switch off your phone? *Meri phaad dee tune. Neil kee toh waat lagee hai.* Ever since you left, we haven't slept. I kept an eye on him like a stupid girl because you wanted me to. He was only concerned for you."

There was no response from the other side. Itishree kept talking for a minute further before she realized the line had been disconnected. She called her again; there was a ring, but no one picked up the phone.

Gauri, on the other hand, packed all her stuff in a jiffy. She called up at the reception to get her car near the main door in ten minutes.

'Neil, here is what I wish to let you know as I come to you. I troubled you enough, I know. I made a fool of you by running away from the situation that I should have braved. But I chickened out. I trusted Arya. Big time. Itishree had warned me. I know for a fact that she is damn possessive about you and therefore she tried to paint a bad image of you. I just took this break as it had all become much for me to come to terms with. This weed did something to me and I could not think straight. I am high even now. I shall tell you more when we meet. Always know that I love you a lot. And idiot, I am an adult now. Please make love to me tonight. I will now sleep with you in your room. I want to sleep in your arms. With my head on your chest. I want that to happen every night. I want you to love me the way I do. And no matter how busy you are, never stop talking to me. Once again, listen, I love you my Neil. Muaaaaaaaaaaaah.'

Gauri's excitement knew no bounds. She wore Neil's favourite dress. She threw away all the sleeping pills and drugs that she had carried along. She did not tell anyone about her plans. Had Neil not been loyal to her, she would have simply killed herself. As she stepped out, she began to kiss the air.

I feel liberated. I feel like I have achieved everything in life.

She wanted to call Itishree again after she started to drive. But the battery had conked off. She had forgotten her fever and the feeling of sickness almost left her body.

❖

I waited for us to meet Itishree. She called me on my cellphone. She sounded nervous but her first statement was that she had spoken with Gauri. She simply said that she kept trying her number and it reached her and she spoke and after that it was not reachable, but Gauri confirmed that she was heading back. I could not believe it at first. I asked her a few times again and then screamed out loud. I could not control my emotions. I found that so soothing and calming that I forgot everything. I immediately informed Dhanya, who smiled at me.

I tried to call Gauri too, but her number could not be reached.

"Why couldn't she tell us before? Now that we ourselves have cracked the case, they are opening their mouth. What about your ex? Did she not call yet?" Dhanya said irritatingly.

"Nahi yaar."

By this time, it was known to us that Arya and Itishree had some connection with this entire case of Gauri's vanishing act.

Whatever it was, I kept questioning why. The puzzle wouldn't last long as we reached to meet Itishree.

"Why did you come down to Neil's house a dozen times?"

Itishree broke down completely. She narrated the entire incident that sent shivers down my spine.

"Oh fuck, you were spying on me? Why the fuck could you not tell me this before? Why did you let everything just happen? How is she now? I am extremely worried about her. How is she now, tell me, Iti...tell..."

I kept shaking Itishree physically and she did not utter a word after that. All that Gauri had told her was that she was in some resort in Lonavla and now she had already planned her return. Itishree had joined us to look for Gauri together.

Dhanya just told me to meet Arya once in case she had some information that the cops wouldn't want to miss.

We kept knocking at her door, but she did not open it. The cops under Dhanya's supervision used force to break the door. The room was stinking with smoke. Her clothes were lying scattered on the floor like she had not remembered taking them off.

And those were taken off one by one. As it also led us into the bathroom where Arya lay in the pool of bloody water. We immediately got her out of the tub. I put the robe around her. Dhanya checked her pulse to discover that she was alive. We did not say anything and had an ambulance take her away. Dhanya collected her laptop, papers, pen and some other stuff that could be of use to her for the investigation. She looked at the papers carefully and read the contents out to me. The picture was almost clear.

I could not stop cursing Arya. There was no sympathy for her.

Itishree realized that this was bigger than what she could have ever imagined. She had waited for us in the gypsy and seeing the ambulance, she jumped out. She began to cry the moment she saw Arya being taken away. She was in utter shock.

I comforted her. Even though I was myself not in the right frame of mind, yet I appeared to be the one who had the hang of the situation.

Dhanya completed her formalities, spoke with Vishwa and we started off for Lonavla.

Itishree kept giving out all the details on the way. I kept listening to her and thinking about Gauri. I called up my parents and even spoke to Gauri's, assuring them.

I began to think of Gauri. Only my heaven knows in the last twenty-four hours, what she was to me. I could not believe how close I had come to her. She meant the world to me. These hours tested me for everything. These hours had been unforgettable. Forgivable, yes.

Her smile kept crossing my mind. The first day when she had met me in the library, our conversation had continued to the college canteen. The games that she loved to play with me. The way she looked at me. The way she and I felt for each other. And the way she would call me 'my Neil'. My tears won't stop. I was in a hurry. I wanted to hold my girl once again in my arms. I wished she had not misunderstood me. I so wish she had spoken to me about it. But that's okay, what has happened has happened. I was quite sure that this would get us closer now.

Dhanya scolded Itishree on the way. The latter remained quiet.

G auri was in no mood to let anyone overtake her. Today was supposedly the most joyous day for her. She had turned Aerosmith on. Her diary was kept on the front seat. She did not keep it in the bag. She kept writing wherever she would face even slight traffic and had to halt her speed for some time.

'I love you Neil. Hope you forgive me one last time. Oh lord, Bryan Adams, you are just in time.

It still feels like our first night together
Feels like the first kiss
It's getting better baby
No one can better this
Still holding on
You're still the one
First time our eyes met
Same feeling I get
Only feels much stronger
I want to love you longer
Do you still turn the fire on?
So if you're feeling lonely, don't
You're the only one I'll ever want
I only want to make it good

So if I love you, a little more than I should
Please forgive me, I know not what I do
Please forgive me, I can't stop loving you
Don't deny me, this pain I'm going through
Please forgive me, if I need you like I do
Please believe me, every word I say is true
Please forgive me, I can't stop loving you
Still feels like our best times are together
Feels like the first touch....

'I don't want these tears to stop. I don't want this love to fade. I don't want this moment to halt. I want to keep going because I have you my Neil.

'I knew that you are not disloyal to me. Always know that. I still did this to never lose you in case there was something. I wanted Arya to step aside forever as she was a strong force who could have possibly screwed my life later on. She wasn't an easy girl to fight with. So I took this necessary step that could help the cops reach out to her as well for her misdeeds should be well exposed. I knew if I were there, I wouldn't necessarily hold on to the ground well.

'I know I had asked Itishree to keep an eye on you. That bloody possessiveness does not go away so easily. I did not want to take a chance. Not even 1% and therefore for that 1% that I goofed up, I seek your forgiveness Neil.

'O God...no...no...Neil...Neil...God....'

"Why the heck is there so much traffic at the turn?" I asked.

One of the constables got down to find out.

"Looks like there is a truck that has overturned about a few metres away."

"That's what, when we want something real bad, there is something that will delay it."

My patience was running thin.

I kept walking. I gradually picked up pace. The trucks, trailers, cars and bikes were all neatly tucked on the side of the road. My feet were leaping. I could hear people talking on the way. People were out on the road. It was a big one.

"Looks like a big accident."

"Arey kaafee log upar gaye shiva shiva shiva"

"Truck aur teen cars ki clash hui hai."

"Ek ladkee akeli thhee uskee car toh full gayi and ladki bhee."

I stopped there and asked the guys. They told me they had gone up the road and figured the accident was real bad. Everybody had died. I just began to run. I kept talking to myself.

"No, it can't be you, Gauri. No, no way! It can't be you!"

I was panting heavily and was about a hundred metres away from the spot of the accident. My vision blurred as perspiration blocked my eyes.

"Are you sure there was a girl in the car?" I asked a stranger. He simply nodded. From about fifty metres, I could see Gauri's car. I was down on the ground. I was motionless. The sun was pouring direct light into my eyes, but I was least reactive. I only could hear whisper around me.

"Looks like she was his wife..."

"That car *na*...he was rushing towards that car..."

"Oh that girl... she was driving with loud music and singing too...I saw that. The truck hit her right in the front and she was screaming 'God and Neil'..."

I did not regain consciousness till I was lifted by the cops back into the gypsy.

When I began to open my eyes, I was in the hospital. Gauri was declared dead. I had died with her. My spirits had died with her.

So I kept looking at her, hoping she would open her eyes. I kept holding her hands like she would get up and hug me. I was in a shell. Completely quiet. I deafened out to all the cries of Itishree, her parents and everyone. I don't know what it was.

I was weeping holding her hands. I did not want to leave. I kept talking to her. I talked to her at length. I asked her what she wanted to have for lunch. She must be tired after her college off site. I had plans. I put the watch that I had bought for her birthday around her wrist. I called up the organising team to ensure all the birthday arrangements were intact. I know I could not do much when you had turned eighteen, but I hope that you would love this surprise. I also got upset in between with her. I asked her to promise me that she would never be gone for so long. I also complained to her that when I had been away, I tried to call but she was not reachable. So now I would buy her a new phone and another connection. I kept talking. She smiled. She promised she wouldn't repeat it.

"Gauri, do you even have an idea what I was going through without you. My Gauri. I was so shit scared. But you know what, I was confident that you would return. I had faith in god. So I was sure he wouldn't let anything bad happen to you. You are my lifeline. You know what, I am serious now. You are not allowed to venture out without letting me know. Don't kill me. I was so freaking helpless in the last twenty-four hours; I was numb. Thanks to all our friends. They worked day and night to find you. Dhanya, come... see Gauri is thanking you. Iti, come... see what you girls were up to. Iti, stop this craziness now... you girls are adults. Every time you do something like this, my heart weakens. Now I can sleep happily in your arms... now I can sleep happily...happily...h...a...p...p...i..."

"Neil, I'm very very sorry man. I can't imagine what has happened. Neil..."

"He is not in his senses. Still reeling under the brutal shock like us," said Itishree, while crying out loud.

"I can't believe this has happened. Just a couple of days ago, we were so happy and excited and planning our life forward. And now this."

Life is a crazy bitch. It is still not known who remains happy here. If at all there is happiness, then it is no guarantee that it shall last forever. It is absolutely fine for God to balance the world, however it is hard to believe how often he cuts those chords of pleasures and gains. The moment you begin to feel joyful, half the life goes worrying about how soon the sorrows might strike you. Now we attribute it to karma or whatever, the big disconnect is if someone like Gauri who did no harm to anyone had to meet a tragic end like this, where does faith go? At these moments, it simply walks out of the door. Keep the faith alive, or keep the hope, or after everything that goes wrong, there is goodness that comes around, is all easier said than done.

Gosh! These moments when a life leaves you without a hint; when your soul mate just flies away far from you to never return; these moments of agony cause you unimaginable grief.

Tom had been standing to my left and Itishree to my right. They must have been in this position for long. Everything else that followed determined humanity. The bed needed to be vacated. Someone else will take that position for commercial purposes. Paper signing would begin. Then people will begin to call Gauri a body. You will only show your helplessness. People kept coming and going. That continued. Gauri had no clue how much she was loved by people. Thousands had turned up. From the college, her school in Guwahati, her gym folks, her food delivery folks, our residential society residents, amongst several others.

Gauri's lip gloss was melting and her foundation had got stuck to her wounded face, so now she had stopped smiling. I think she was gone now. It was all gone. I was down to the real world. World sans beauty.

Tom grabbed me tight. I burst into tears. I only cried. Louder and louder. I kept talking to Tom and Gauri intermittently. Only Tom was responding. He consoled me the best he could. This was the first major setback in my life. And this lasted forever.

Few days later, I stretched my eyes out of the window. I hadn't done it in a while. I wasn't talking to the palm anymore. I had asked it to keep my life happy with Gauri. It had let me down. It failed miserably. I could see that palm was not able to look at me eye to eye. Just like Itishree. They let me down one way or the other. Not just the two of them, even god and I had a break up for now.

I prepared breakfast for Gauri, put it on the table. Yet again. Drew the curtains because I wanted no shadow of it to fall on my beautiful Gauri. Coaxed her into finishing it. She didn't seem to be hungry. She told me that she had her exams and that's why she was kind of worried. I hugged and kissed her. I told her about the plans for her birthday celebrations. She was excited.

The doorbell rang but I could not hear it at first. I was lost in my love. The visitor must have easily spent ten minutes at the door. It must be someone very close to me. Who waits these days for you? Nobody waits. People leave you.

"Neil, I did not bother you in last few days. Here are some of Gauri's possessions that we found in the car. I just want to hand it over to you. As a protocol, I am supposed to give this to her parents, but I didn't tell them all about it. You may decide what you want to keep and what you want to give to them."

"Dhanya, why did this happen to me? Why on earth did I fail?"

"Time heals all wounds. Life needs to move on. You can't torture and blame yourself as that would hurt Gauri more. Understand she is always with you. She is a part of you now. So you got to take care of yourself. Her diary might kill you further. Sorry I had to read it for any clues and evidence. I really wanted to round up Arya. Gauri mentioned that she should be forgiven as she is human. Since there is no case filed here, I leave that decision to you. Anyway, spoken enough, tell me what do you have to say? Don't keep shut, please talk to me, Neil."

"I completely understand, Gauri... sorry, I mean Dhanya. I am screwed....insanity has bitten me. Is it in our hands really to control our heartbeat? Or to make it beat or stop when we want? No, right? So whatever is going with me is not driven by me. So far as Arya goes, if Gauri wants her to be forgiven, so be it. Whatever Gauri has decided shall always take priority. By the way, again, thank you Dhanya. I know you need to focus on your wedding. Just ensure all goes well."

"Parson aayenge hum shadi ka card lekar." Dhanya's emotions indicated how awful she was feeling.

❖

It was a reclusive night. She played the video on her laptop. All the memories of her childhood days flashed. All of it in front of her eyes. Soaked eyes. She was feeling the screen with her trembling fingers. Itishree was heart-wrenched. She was drawn into a cocoon. She had not stepped out of the house.

Partly also because she was feeling guilty and felt that she could have avoided all that had happened. Her situation had worsened in the last five days. She had not been talking to anyone either.

She watched the videos in haphazard order. Sometimes as a child playing with Gauri and other times when they were in the college. Then the video that Gauri had recorded for Itishree popped up.

Remember Iti, when we were in high school, we used to talk about our crushes. I had Neil but you did not spare Salman Khan. You were mad, like real mad for him. Then I gifted you his posters from Maine Pyaar Kiya *and* Baaghi.

One day I will make you meet him, I promise. And when Neil and I get married, we will invite him over. Maybe Sallu gets hooked up with you then. And listen, when you are watching this video, just turn around, I am right behind you.

Itishree immediately turned around. It was the wall with her poster smiling at Itishree.

The distance between the two girls was non-existent. They seemed conjoint. Itishree spent all these days like this. In the memories.

She had put Gauri's photographs on the walls of her bedroom. She had started wearing her perfume, her clothes. She began to do everything that Gauri had ever complained to her of. Then she found out a few joints stashed under her mattress. She immediately took them out and crushed them in wild anger. That reminded her of the dreadful night. Itishree lost her cool. She started taking out Arya's name in anger that she had never expressed before.

"You bitch, you whore, you could not handle him and you fucking screwed our lives now. You killed my sister. You fuckin' killed her. You first tried to kill her innocence and then you got her hooked on to this stupid stuff. She was not in her senses when she drove away. It's all because of you that she is not with me anymore!

"You killed a life when it was beginning to live. You killed a dream when it was waiting to turn into reality. You killed a girl who was going to be a woman. You killed a bride. You killed me. You killed my soul. You are a mass murderer. Even a grave is not the right place for you to hide.

"I was such a fool not to have known what will happen to Gauri. She was under severe depression and she thought she was happy with you."

Itishree held Gauri's pictures in her hand and kept talking to her after hurling abuses in the air in Arya's name.

Then the doorbell distracted her. The delivery contained two dresses that Gauri had sent for them both to be worn for the party night.

Itishree sat down wearing it the whole night and the whole of the next day.

She was not able to get over the feeling of loneliness, denial and seclusion.

"Why would you leave me here to die? Why shouldn't I be there when I was always there with you in all your car races, your adventures, your freaky life! And then, all your friends who became mine too, left me in the confines of this college. Do you have any clue, Gauri, how difficult it is for me to attend any class, any college thing? Do you have an idea of how I feel sitting alone on the bench in the class, library or canteen. Well, I just do it out of compulsion. You know why? So I don't hurt your soul. You'd always say that we should do what we feel like, what we feel good about. So I am still trying to figure that. The only time of the day I love the most is when I look at the sky and talk to you. And my favourite star up there is you. I am fixed on it. That apart, nothing is working out yaar. Gauri, please come back yaar. Please. I am very alone.

"And I have been looking for Neil all these days. There is no clue. I tried to enquire at college, cops, his family, nobody knows anything about him and I am shocked that nobody wants to find out either. It would only imply that they don't want to tell me. How on earth is it possible that Neil's parents don't know where he is. I know he is a great guy and therefore I am much keen on knowing about him. Just for you. Just for keeping your life going in my heart. Your life cannot stop with that one mishap.

"Neil – you have to return. You better show up soon. It is absolutely unfair for a so-called man to be vanishing. You can't chicken out. If I am braving it, and doing it all by myself, then why can't you. At least for Gauri's sake you should have come back. She won't forgive you, Neil. I am telling you, she is my soulmate before she even got in a relationship with you. I know her more, and this way, you are hurting her more.

"Gauri, why don't you ask your Neil to show up. I need to tell him a lot about you. Things that he hadn't known. Things that you always wanted to do. All that you loved.

"Gauri, I also want to tell you that I want to do all those things that you wanted to do yourself and also for me to achieve. I want you to grow in my skin, Gauri. I know you would do that beautifully well. A part of you is anyway in me. I miss you, my love. I miss you, my honey."

Itishree kept repeating these words before falling off to sleep.

❖

She was relieved from the hospital a day before. Her parents were informed of her condition but surprisingly nobody turned up to see her. Arya was all alone. She had turned pale. Her frail look was a result of drug overdose, and all the torture she had made her body go through.

She rolled a joint. Then, she sat in front of the mirror and began with a soliloquy.

"I had made a grave blunder of leaving you, Neil. I wanted you to come around. I wanted you to apologise for not being able to take out time for me as much as I wanted. I always believed you'd do it. But I was wrong. I want you back in my life. Badly. Now your love is no more. Can you come back to me? I really want you. See, I have nobody around me. Everyone has left me. I, me, myself. Hahahaha...mercy!

"Gauri,may your soul rest in peace. You were a real good girl. You were actually a real good girl. You died, but why did you not die peacefully? Why did you die like this? You created a complete ruckus. Now, this man is neither yours nor mine, and that is what I had feared the most."

She began to puff in vigorously. Then she went near the mirror again.

"Bitch! You were one, Gauri. Gauri..."

With huge force, she broke the mirror. She did that multiple times. Breaking the pieces. Shards flew across on the floor. Screaming and crying, she passed out.

❖

Itishree called me. I did not pick the phone. Like I mentioned earlier. I wasn't willing to talk to her. It is not that I did not feel like it. It is not that I did not feel like forgiving her. I did. But I could not deliver the forgiveness to her. In a way, I allowed penance. I don't know whether I was right or wrong. But at that moment, I was more than right based on what I was going through. During my time of healing, I was left alone, given space by Tom. He was clear. He knew me extremely well. He knew I believed that time heals all wounds. I was healing. Or maybe I will begin to heal. Whatever it was, he was there for me in his and my thoughts.

As the night gloomed in, I stepped out to the balcony like my daily ritual. I waved at the stars and said hello to Gauri. I had shifted from talking to the palm tree to talking to the stars now. She was one of those. I was certain.

To me the oneness with the night was reason to be with her.
To me the oneness with the universe was reason because I loved her.
The starry skies showered the love back to me.
More than I deserve for it was at the direction of Gauri.
To me those lengthy discussions with the stars meant something.
That Gauri would never leave me for anything.
One day I shall amalgamate with her deeper in the skies.
To me the oneness with the universe was reason to be with her again.

We cracked jokes, we laughed out loud. In a long time, I was this happy. She kept hiding behind her friends and then she would hide behind those clouds. I hated the clouds. But then she would show up again. Gauri, you haven't changed a bit. You always win at hide and seek. But this time, I will win. Because I found you again.

Come on Neil, how could you win. I was to your left and you were looking to your right.

You always have the last laugh baby.

Yeah, my Neil.

I was exhausted after the game of hide and seek. I asked Gauri to have her dinner as we had a long day tomorrow.

She was stubborn. She was not willing to listen to me. She seemed to be up to some other mischief. I let her be there. I told the clouds clearly to move out of the way as I would come back again to talk to my Gauri. Up there in the sky of diamonds.

I went to my room and began to read all the letters that she had written while she was in the resort. That was my toughest night. That night I actually felt that I was living for no reason. Or rather I was only alive with Gauri. I literally had a piercing pain in my chest that cracked through the heart. My heart was filled with heaviness and eyes were out of focus. What else could I do? Except to wail in anguish.

I had Gauri's pictures spread all over the bed. Though I did not need to, as she was always near me. Yet I did it this way. The reason was because these pictures were all from her childhood till the present.

Gauri, I so much wish that I could hold you in my arms, like so close.

I never stopped you Neil.

Thanks, my love. I want to wrap you around me tonight.

Go ahead darling

That voice does it all to me, your skin I just love to feel, your body I love to smell, you are sensuous; you simply turn me on.

And I love the way you make me feel loved. It's the way you make me feel that matters to me the most, my man.

Come... sssshhhhhhh...just come closer to me as I undress you.

Aaahhhh...it's so special...your touch is so special. Look at my breasts...they are craving to be in your mouth. Suck them, bite them, lick them.

Yes love...umm....why are you so goddamn hot!

Gauri began to undress me.

She loved to remain on top for a long time. She began to kiss me harder. That French kiss transcended me into a different world. She got up slowly and slowly she held my hair, and then with a jerk, pulled them back and then came down on my face and the mouth and bit my lips. I kept moving my hands on her back and went down to squeeze her bum. She bent down. I used my fingers to feel her vagina. Then I turned her around. Her breasts were in my mouth again. I gently bit her nipples. She began to moan and moved her body, swirled it like she was completely ecstatic. I kissed her naval while moving my hands on her thighs. The foreplay lasted about thirty minute before we were spent.

I opened my eyes and realized it was dark. I held her close in my arms and went to sleep. I slept for the first time in the last week.

Gauri did not leave my hands even for a moment that night.

❖

I woke up and as usual made breakfast for her. But today I could not see her. I opened the window and it was bright sun that shone in. So I would only meet her in the night. I sat down, talked to her, imagining she was having breakfast with me. Well, that's what I have been doing for the last one week. Her room was made up in no time. Her pictures were cleaned. She was finicky about cleanliness. The reason why we had sanitized the house.

The post-it sticky notes were replaced with my ink in her handwriting. The weather forecast was noted. Gym fees was paid. That meant I had stepped out of the house? The answer is no. I sent cash through the pizza delivery boy. Why pizza? Wondering? Because it was on our agenda to have some together. He remembered Gauri fondly. Got emotional seeing me. Before he left, he simply said, "Sir, you please take care of yourself. And...sir...we miss ma'am a lot."

Tom showed up. He had to. No intimation. No phone call.

"Your 'me' time is up. Come, let's go for some food."

He spotted pizza and like a brother understood it all. "Okay, Gauri, you, and I will go for a drive. We shall take the pizza with us."

I was happy hearing that. He drove and talked. That day he must have spoken the maximum with me. He stopped on the way. We both stepped out.

"I have to give this to you." Tom looked at me, cross eyed.

"What's in it?" I asked as a quick reaction.

"Since when have you started believing in this?"

"Prayers heal. Keep this with you."

I did not argue with him. Not because my break up with god was over. But there is something in a friendship that always remain intact. Trust. Belief. And often times, just because your friend is asking you to.

"How could Arya have befriended Gauri in a matter of a week to this extent? Even after so many years, we remain sensitive to each other. Even if she was faking it, didn't she even think of her once?"

"Start praying. Start meditating. You shall have all the answers. You need to converse more with the universe now. Use it as much as you'd like. And remember, god still exists. And now, Gauri is one too," Tom said pointing at the box and then raising his head towards the sky. I watched along.

"I know, I spoke with her last night. She is happily missing me," I said, giving a tight hug to my bestie.

He dropped me back. He asked me for a promise; that whatever I planned to do, I needed to keep him informed. We did not talk about Itishree at all. I was expecting him to, but he did not. That suggested one thing – he had he met her and hence he would have known that I was still upset with her. More now in a conscious state of mind. Simple friends stuff yet again, not to do what the other person wouldn't like.

I made the promise to him.

My evening was a replica of the previous one. As night crawled over, I was in my magnificent world with Gauri. We were in a similar romantic moment as we had been in the previous night. I don't know what exactly happened but I woke up with a jerk. I felt kind of weirdly uncomfortable. I had never experienced this before. Being loved and to love your girl should not be shocking. I turned on the lights, reached the prayer book and chanted some hymns. It was not by design or by necessity or by choice that I reached out for the prayers. It was not instinct driven. It was some divine force that I felt, powerful enough to lead me to the books.

I wondered why. But slowly some thoughts began to form a zone inside me. I don't think I was attracted only physically towards Gauri that I had to get lust to overpower my love. I had somehow felt so this time around that what I was doing was not right. I simply began to pray. I told Gauri that my love for her was pure and devoid of any lust. Then I wondered why I missed her physically so much. I had my answers. I was completely distracted. I needed peace of mind. At this point, it was haywire. I had to decide what I really wanted in life, provided Gauri was always an integral part of it.

I sat at the bus stop for a long time. I watched people walking, shopping, talking and doing all the 'ings' that could well be spotted. This was way too different than Pune. This was more like a discovery for me. Like I didn't know what my country has to offer. The purpose had got me here. Though I was still three kilometres away from my final destination, McLeod Ganj. I was at Dharamshala.

It took me five days to reach here. It is not that my life had changed drastically over these five days and I had come to Himachal for a holiday. You would be able to certainly guess that my purpose would be different. More so from what had happened that night five days ago before my departure from Pune. Well, that was my permanent departure from Pune.

From the Gulmohar and Ashoka to the Deodhar. From the Sahyadri mountain ranges to the Dhauladhar ranges.

It ain't an easy shift for someone. For me, I had no other option left. I was getting venomous. I was losing track. My mind was warped. I was seeing her all the time. Also, she was becoming an object at times. An object that I could use per my whims and fancies. An object that I would treat with sympathy. Worse of all, an object to fulfill my carnal desires.

So for me, the shift was mandatory. I had a choice prior to making it. To give up, to give into...what was that? Of course it was irking me. On my way to Dharamshala, when I was only a few minutes away, I could not stop from asking a fellow who appeared Buddhist to me. In fact, he was. As I drew my vision closer to him, I became certain that he was a monk.

"Sir, I wish to give up. I wish to give into circumstances. I have no hope, no desires, no charm left of living my life anymore. I lost my world two weeks ago." I shared my story with him in five minutes. I had been waiting all these days to let it out.

He looked at me, smiled, blessed me and said, "'Give up' and 'give into' should change to 'give to'. Start giving to people. See the happiness on their faces. Start giving to nature and see the happiness in the universe. Bless you."

We got down at the bus stop. I chased him. He stopped and asked me, "You have come here to find all the answers. I can tell you, you shall find them all. Meet me tomorrow near the temple."

Then he left and I returned to the stop. That temple was in McLeod Ganj.

I moved to the toll booth and called up Tom. He broke down completely.

"*Teri bahut yaad aati hai bhai. Aunty aur uncle ko bhee daily phone kar lena.* We all love you. And listen, I am not in contact with Itishree. I know it won't matter to you. But she kept on asking me about you. She has given me the recordings of Gauri's videos ever since she was a child."

"*Kya bol raha hai,* Tom? You are simply making me cry. It hurts. I can't get over Gauri. I wish I could forgive Itishree. I feel guilty of being rude to her. I will see you soon. Once I find my answers."

We chatted for a few minutes before I hung up.

I took the last bus to McLeod Ganj.

Nestled in the Dhauladhar range, with a beautiful high peak behind, McLeod Ganj in Kangra valley speaks for the beautiful culture of Tibetan Buddhism. The place boasts of spiritual and cultural tourism. I was in complete awe of it. My first few days were spent visiting the monasteries and trying to discover myself.

I spent much time at Tsuglag Khang or Dalai Lama temple. My purpose was simple. I wanted to shun all evil that I might carry and also gain spirituality.

Everything seemed so calm and serene. It did remind me of the northeast, the place where I hailed from.

After spending a few days, came my calling. I joined a Buddhism course. I met the monk. His name was Junko. He was a bright scholar and every word he spoke had such deep-rooted meaning.

We spoke about the mind, emotions and karma at length. In fact, there were two courses I had undergone. I realized that Buddhism is a philosophy more than a religion. It is a way of life. I had begun to like it.

One day, while I was talking to Junko, I told him about my anger with Itishree. He simply shared a beautiful story on anger that I could never forget.

"A woman who practices reciting Buddha Amitabha's name, is very tough, and recites 'Namo Amitabha Buddha' three times daily. Although she has been doing this practice for over ten years, she is still quite mean, shouting at people all the time. She starts her practice by lighting incense and then hitting a little bell.

"A friend wanted to teach her a lesson, and just as she began her recitation, he came to her door and called out, 'Miss Nuyen, Miss Nuyen!'

"As this was the time for her practice, she got annoyed, but she said to herself: 'I have to struggle against my anger, so I will just ignore it.'

"And she continued, 'Namo Amitabha Buddha, Namo Amitabha Buddha...'

"But the man continued to shout her name, and she became more and more agitated.

"She struggled against it and wondered if she should stop the recitation to give the man a piece of her mind, but she continued reciting, 'Namo Amitabha Buddha, Namo Amitabha Buddha...'

"The man outside heard it and continued, 'Miss Nuyen, Miss Nuyen...'

"Then she could not stand it anymore, jumped up, slammed the door and went to the gate and shouted, 'Why do you have to behave like that? I am doing my practice and you keep on shouting my name over and over!'

The gentleman smiled at her and said,"I just called your name for ten minutes and you are so angry. You have been calling Amitabha Buddha's name for more than ten years now; just imagine how angry he must be by now!'"

I was enthralled by this story. In such a simple manner, with such a deep meaning. That is what the teachings are all about. What I learned in my school and was learning in my college would probably fetch me a job. What I was learning would make me successful. Reading and learning outside the curriculum about life matters a lot. I did not know that significantly earlier.

The lessons were great. The teachings were efficacious. The transformation was in progress.

I knew there would be disruptions, there would be distractions, but I held on. Not as simple as it may sound. The universe has some powers and I had begun to realize it. Those powers heal you. But then, not like you talk and it works. That works when you are willing to be healed. Hence it's not as simple as it sounds. The tricky part is when we are broken, we forget if there is any healing left in the world. So this thing called universe comes into play. I was in regular touch with it as I had come closer here, amongst the spiritual monks, in the greens and mountains, near the moon and the stars. Near Gauri. Near my universe. So it was healing me.

Over next few days, I got into reading books. They had an excellent library. I was impressed. It contained books from the spectra that one could only imagine. Reading books has the most wonderful process of calming your senses. It is meditative, soothing and what not.

I would be a naive to say that I was becoming some sort of a spiritual guru myself. At first, that is the impression one would draw. But trust me, I was far from that. The only point was that my intentions were strong. It was a pristine form of process. I was in it. After I would read a part of the book, I would do some work around cleaning the books in the library, washing the place et al. Then the prayers were a regular feature. Come night, and I would gaze at the stars. And I can confidently reassure you that Gauri was happier. Much of what it was leading to had to do with her. She gave me the strength to learn to breath again.

She helped me deal with my fears. So when I was forming myself into a much desired state, she would acknowledge. I spoke with her, waved and returned to my room.

Whatever I had learned, helped me connect with myself and the universe at a spiritual level. So it was oneness with the universe. Oneness with Gauri, as she was now the universe. I was more at ease in conversing with her. Precisely why I did not talk about her in the last thirty days. She was now connected. The conversations were through the heart. She was doing much better now on the other side. She seemed liberated too. I could see that in the sky. The star kept blinking at me. Like she was now that fulfilling star. She didn't need to have the stars falling for me; she was good enough. Thirty days ago, I simply asked her to be on my side. Now she was. The distance had shortened. She lived in my heart. She will always be my girl. In the last thirty days, I did not speak with anyone at home. But they were on my mind. I had prayers for everyone in my life.

So I decided to talk to everyone one by one. Okay, in short, I learned to be aware of the situations, to understand how happiness can be attained despite pain and suffering and also how to practice good karma. I won't say I had reached the level of awakening, however I had gained some ground.

Today, when I speak to all, I might sound composed and different. I might sound like a man to my dad, a good son to my mom, a compassionate friend to Tom and truthful to god.

Just when I reached the phone booth, my limbs trembled. I got worried. Why would this happen to me? I thought my learning was temporary. If I had achieved a sense of peace, then the pleasures should not impact me so much that I get drawn into emotions.

I hurriedly returned to the temple. My monk guru simply smiled and did not ask me anything. I did not tell him anything either. How do I tell him that I feel I have failed? How do I tell him that I only find myself successful when I am around him or in the temple? How do I tell him that I might have let him down?

While the barrage of questions hit me hard, there was no way I could be dishonest to him either.

I thought about asking him the next day. That night I tried hard to sleep, but could only do so for a couple of hours.

The next morning I woke up to a letter that was pushed under my door. And what it taught me was something that I would never forget.

Buddhism teaches that wisdom should be developed with compassion. At one extreme, you could be a good-hearted fool and at the other extreme, you could attain knowledge without any emotion. Buddhism uses the middle path to develop both. The highest wisdom is seeing that in reality, all phenomena are incomplete, impermanent and do not constitute a fixed entity. True wisdom is not simply believing what we are told but instead experiencing and understanding truth and reality. Wisdom requires an open, objective and unbigoted mind. The Buddhist path requires courage, patience, flexibility and intelligence.

So be patient. Be prepared. Be open. Everything else shall fall in place. Also, never forget that your learning is a part of you. With each experience of your life, at some point you shall begin to reflect those. Just hold on. Now go back to where you belong. And last but not the least, don't stop giving.

Junko.

I carried it. I was looking for Junko. I asked people around me about his whereabouts. Nobody had a clue. Nobody knew. I was inquisitive. So I went to the temple and met the monk who used to sit with us in the prayer area. He told me that he had always seen me alone. He had seen me praying alone. So there was nobody called Junko. Nobody by that name out there. I looked up in the sky, and said, "Gauri, I shall last as long as you do. I shall last forever. Thanks, Junko."

I am of the firm belief that when life gives you pain, less of it or lots of it, it gives you strength to face it too. The option lies within us. Either we could leverage to the fullest or give up. Some of us give up, some confide in best friends and family and a lot many keep trying to ignore it. If I have to fit myself in this scenario, I do not fall in any of these. I have bravely faced all my pains. Does that make me rare? Not really, because people who can ignore the pain only have two sides to it – one, who keep suffering and ignore fearing the consequences if they face it. By that logic, there are others who are able to ignore it as they do not feel it worthy enough to pay heed to. They are able to face it, overcome it as they are strong mentally and emotionally. That's what I have been aiming for. Not to endure the pain, but to become further strong mentally and emotionally.

It had been close to three years that I had left the arms of Himachal Pradesh for my studies. But there isn't a single year when I don't visit the temples at McLeod Ganj. During the last two visits, I had a full gang who was part of the trip. Jerry was the first one to join it. Ever since, each class gifted me with several friends. Tom always remained special and Jerry formed the complete trio. You make friends in college based on many presumptions and needs. Few of those are:

a) We belong to the same town. Smaller the town, stronger the friendship.

b) We scored similar marks in school and therefore got admission in the same college.

c) We have the same class, same taste for smokes, liquor, girls and madness.

d) We have similar passions in life – music, art, literature, travel, et al.

e) We carry broken hearts, pain and sorrow and endless agony.

I did strike off my friendships from second year onwards based on the above. While nobody could replace Tom, there was a small bunch that got hooked to me owing to my travels

137

and other stuff. Being the capital of India, you had all the means of transport to travel anywhere in the country. Of all the places, Himachal, though it sounds distant, was also like next door.

❖

It was the computer lab where I was spending my day today. This was adjacent to the girls' hostel. Unbelievably true, but some boys opted for the course, so they could smell the perfumes and even peep around the hostel. Everything could be considered possible in colleges. I was deeply engrossed in my subject. The activities in the campus were building up. All thanks to the upcoming Engifest which was scheduled for 20th February. This was a phenomena every year at our college of engineering. Jerry came running to me. He pulled me out of the lab instantly.

"What happened, *kaminey? Aise kyu uthha laaya mujhe?*"

"Did you know this time we have a glamour section in our fest?"

"What is that?"

"Neil, you are part of the committee. I am asking you as I believe you would have all the answers."

"Bro, you know more than anyone else here. You are a full *khabri!*"

"Yes, I know there are Miss India contestants coming from different colleges this time around to participate in the ramp walk. That would give our DCE a definite boost up. Media is also covering the event. What else would you like to know?"

"*Yahooo...tu is baar koi set kar le bro.* Gauri would be the happiest if you do so. Please!" Jerry crossed his eyes, gave me that pleasing look which he brings out once in a quarter. And like every time, I walked away.

We were two days away from the fest. Many performers had taken over the campus. Looked like Wembley Stadium preparing to host Aerosmith. Rehearsals were in full steam and ran well all over the place. I sat down on the bench near the amphitheater and carefully observed the hustle bustle. From that distance, all I could notice was that everyone was working. Except me. Not really, I just took a break. I was guiding the juniors on how to welcome the guests. But then I realized they were way too smart. They almost befriended them during their practice hours. I did not need to do much except conduct mild supervisions. Advantages of being a senior.

Amidst all the interesting activities, a girl kept looking at me from a distance. I noticed from the corner of my eye. Then I stretched my eyes in direct contact. To me it seemed that her legs were longer than Jerry's height. Her hair reached her waist. She was certainly one of the performers. I had never seen her before. She looked like Claudia Schiffer at the helm of her modeling career. Before I could observe anything further, she left a dazzling smile and then disappeared.

I was expecting Tom any moment now. Every year around the fest, he would plan his visit to me. Like my dearest friend, he made his entry just in time. Because, I was about to doze off. I was still sitting on the bench. The sun was shooting its raging rays into my eyes as I was too lazy to turn to the other side. Who would mind the sun in the chill of a February day in Delhi.

"Neil, tell me something. Why do I see you here on this bench every time I arrive?"

Tom and I didn't leave each other's embrace for a long time. That's how it had been for years when we meet after a gap. The gap had widened now. He always questions me why I never returned to Pune. Why I never even revisited Pune after the Himachal trip? Why did I run away from everything that reminded me of Gauri?

It was a complex question for me to answer. It isn't true that I did not know the answer or I did not attempt to do so. Especially with Tom, someone who knows me inside out. But it was certainly not easy to answer the same. Remember that I am not a weak soul and I am not the one who would escape the pain. I am a strong man now who is learning to face the world. That standard is set for me. I wasn't always like that. During the course of the journey, I had become an escapist, and later when I evolved, it was late for me to revisit the situation or people. So I always believed that now if I go to Pune, I would be selfish. Because when I should have gone, I did not and now it would be mechanical. So far as Gauri is concerned, she always remained with me like a star that could be viewed from anywhere in the world.

This wasn't easy to explain as it is more philosophical... precisely why I never could do that to Tom.

Tom, Jerry and I spent the next couple of days hanging around. I could see our friendship with Jerry getting stronger. In between I tried to look for the girl, but could not find her. There were far too many people who had thronged the campus, and secondly, I did not know which group she belonged to. Finally, we were not eating in our campus these days. We were only hanging out. So we missed it. Honestly, I also did not broach the subject much. She did last longer in my head, but not to the extent of damaging our happy hours.

The three-day event had now begun. And we knew, like each year, this one would also be a rocking show. College students go mad around this time. Everybody has a talent that emerges in the fests. A couple's romance blooms. Inter college relationships take place. The break-ups get replaced with new lovers. Some hearts break too. All that in the garb of the events is synonymous with the relationships. The final day was more calming and most extravagant. The final event was the ramp walk by the most coveted Miss India participants. It was breathtaking. All stunning beauties on one stage. They turned the fever on. The crowd was going berserk. I saw my girl. My girl, as in the girl who had a short stay in my heart a couple of days ago. I could not take my eyes off her. Of course she wouldn't know now that I was gazing at her; that I was completely into her. She wouldn't know anything. The distance, height of the stage and most of all the flashlights dropping in her eyes separated her vision from mine. Anyway, she was completely focused on her walk. The crowd kept cheering, shouting and dancing. I continued to keep looking. I was flabbergasted. How could anyone look so much like Gauri? How on earth was that possible? Rule of friendship – when in doubt, ask your bestie.

"Tom, stop looking around. What do you think about her?" I asked him, carelessly pointing my fingers at her.

He froze on his chair. He got up and even got closer to the stage.

"Damn! That face looks so much like Gauri. I have seen her. Maybe she is a cousin you never met."

"Quite a possibility, Tom. I really would love to meet her."

"This is your college and you are anyway part of the committee; it is easy for you to find out anything about her."

Jerry returned to his seat after some time. He was gone for long. He pulled me aside mysteriously and I held Tom's hands. Within seconds, all of us were out of the amphitheater.

He looked at me and asked what would I do if he had got the details of Gauri look alike. He said that with greater intensity. Like he had some secret information that would stun us.

"Hahahaha Jerry. We were talking about it and you appeared like a CIA agent."

"What I will tell you now shall otherwise be considered classified information. Nobody in this campus would have got that info."

"Jerry come on, out with it now!" Tom ordered sternly.

"She is Itishree. Pursuing her dental studies from a college in Pune. DYP dental college, to be precise," he continued.

I was stunned. Not stunned, I was shocked. Rather, more than just shocked. So I gradually benumbed. In the world that is governed by destiny, and the learning that I had emulated, this was the best example of how anything could happen anytime. When you expect the least, the most unexpected can occur. I had almost erased Itishree from my memories. I was stubborn about that. Tom followed suit. He also stayed away from her. Like I said earlier, just so that I stay away from any pain. Tom did, because he felt that would hurt me if I knew that he was in touch with her. So it was a friendly compulsion. Certainly, I had no malice that I held in my heart, especially after the McLeod Ganj Buddhism teachings.

Tom got our official photographer around. He asked him to pull out the videos and pictures of the ramp walk. We all sat down and looked at the pictures carefully. It was established, while giving it a cautious glance that she was indeed Itishree who was behaving and looking like Gauri. It was by far, excitingly surprising and I was inquisitive to find out more. This was the moment when I would turn selfish. Itishree was now holding answers to my questions. On the other hand, if I did not find out from her, then it would always haunt me. Because somewhere, it impacted me deeply.

Tom offered to take a lead in this. He knew it would not make any sense for them to act in haste. I agreed. We decided to let her return to Pune. Only once she settled back in, would Tom go and meet her.

He was super cute when he said to me, "*Bhai,* looks like Gauri's soul has entered Itishree. I am not surprised. Let us meet her soon."

"You are there for me, I know. I hope we get this solved," I said, giving it a deep thought.

Three days later

It was on the front page of the mid day paper. Her picture appeared with a caption that she had dropped out of the most coveted Miss India contest. There was a press conference that she had addressed last evening. She was clear that she would need to back out of the event due to personal reasons. The media folks were definitely unhappy and displeased with Itishree. She did not answer anything except stating that the reasons were extremely personal and that she had already spoken with the committee and taken care of contract related things.

Tom was waiting for the weekend so he could visit her college and meet her. But the news shook him to the core. He was now extremely puzzled as to how to approach Itishree. What had happened in last three days? There has to be something drastic. He needed to find out. He tried to meet up with the contest committee chapter of Pune. He had no luck for simple reasons, that the press release was already available that could be accessed and there was nothing beyond what was officially stated. This meant that Tom had to get in touch with Itishree at the earliest. He got a quick contact with her college and then tried to fix a meeting at the earliest. It was simply not easy and it required a lot of persuasion on Tom's part. In fact, it was only Tom who could possibly even attempt to speak with her.

"Yes, Tom what do you want?"

"Iti, how have you been?"

"Itishree...."

"Sorry Iti, I did not get you."

"Itishree...that's my name."

"Oh okay, I am sorry, Itishree. Please do not say no. I want to meet you."

"What do you mean, Tom? Who do you think I am, Tom? How dare you even call me now? What do you think? If Neil was upset, why did you back off? I tried killing myself. I needed you guys with me at that point. And you left me. I felt like a criminal. There has not been a single day when I did not cry. Do you know why I participated in the contest? Do you even have a fucking idea? Do you think I wanted to be Miss India? No! I did that because I was searching for you all. Because I knew all the engineering folks would gather. If not all, some bright ones will. I knew you and Neil would definitely be there. I just knew that. I missed it during the last couple of years. But this time, I was sure. I saw Neil sitting on the bench. I was looking for you all these years..."Itishree broke down and hung up.

Tom did not have the courage for a few minutes to call her back. Tom attempted calling her once again. The reception picked up. They asked him to wait. Then he was told that Itishree was busy. Tom called her a few times till the night set in. Itishree refused to come to attend to his call. He repeated it the next day and then the day after. The result was the same. Tom felt horrible about it.

He called up her parents. They had moved to Siliguri. Fortunately, the new occupants of the house had retained their phone number. Itishree's mom picked up the phone. He was happy about that. He knew that moms are usually kind-hearted and soft and can melt easily. Tom tried that with her and it worked.

She had got sentimental while conversing with Tom. She did not have a son. So whenever a male friend of Itishree would talk to her, she thought of him like her son. She sounded worried after a moment. She told him how Itishree had been broken into damaged pieces after losing Gauri. They even feared that she might take some wrong measures. She had stopped coming to Guwahati as that reminded her of her childhood with Gauri. That's the reason why they had shifted to Siliguri, leaving everything as their daughter meant everything to them. Then Itishree moved out of college and took admission in DYP for a dentistry course. She had become secluded after trying to look for Tom and me. She ran from pillar to post and even tried her best to check with my parents about my whereabouts. How would they tell her when I had kept them in the dark?

Tom swelled with anger for me and guilt for himself. He called me up and vented it out.

"Till when do you think I will be in charge of things that you should be doing? Till when do I follow you even when I find it least convincing to be anywhere near being justified? Tell me Neil. Do you have any answer today?"

"I am flying down to you later tonight. I am checking on the net whether the last flight is available."

Tom hung up. He did not inform Itishree of my plans. Logically, it made sense.

❖

When a girl is angry with you, one of the below might work. In case it does not, then even god can't help you. Yet, try it out.

a) Be quiet when she is upset and/or screaming at you.
b) Offer her a chair to sit on, depending on the location. Not the lap.
c) Act dumb, like you know you screwed up, but you didn't know you ended up screwing it.
d) Let her feel that she has won completely.

All of the above would only work in cases of short-term anger.

But, in this case, it was not just about anger; there was lot of frustration buried in her. Lot of questions and anxiety. When I got to know from Tom that Itishree had attempted killing herself, I considered myself guilty. I prayed to god to forgive me. God had the simple answer that I should seek the same from Itishree. So it was more about genuinely persuading her. I did know that I would not lie to her. It wouldn't be easy to face her. But that is something I was going to put to use now, after learning it from my Buddhist course. Every time there is talk or mention of me, dealing with a tough situation or circumstances, there is no way or reason why I wouldn't talk about my learning at the foothills of Dhauladhar ranges. But the quest always remains. It takes time to be in that state. I believe that's Nirvana.

❖

"How long will you wait, sir? Looks like she does not want to meet you,"said the security guard at the reception.

This was expected. I knew how to convince her. I know it was not the right way, but that was the only way left for me. I told the guard to tell her that there is something about Gauri I have to share with her. It worked. Itishree appeared right in front of me. As if she was watching me from some place close. But that was not the point. It was supposed to hit beyond the normal level of emotions. That obviously meant I had to walk to the place which had the least crowd. This is how you prepare for tears or any emotional upheaval that you are bound to come across.

"Itishree, please do not say anything. Please. Just give me one chance to explain to you. If you still believe and feel that I was wrong, then any punishment is acceptable to me."

I had folded my hands, and my tears had already begun to flow down my cheeks, slightly lesser than Itishree's though. We had Gauri's soul in us and that's what was connecting us to the point of breaking down. We knew the point we had left each other – unfinished talks, zero motivation levels and no desire to live.

"I know I was upset with you. After I had seen the videos of you and Gauri, I was getting sucked deeper into my shell. I would watch them every day and cry. I might have died in my room. Had that situation not happened where I had felt that I was being selfish and using Gauri as an object, I would have never gone to Himachal. If I had come to meet you at that point, I would have never been able to get normal. Meeting or seeing you would have reminded me of her to the point of madness. I wanted to stop. I might have become destructive. Yes, I realized all this while doing the Buddhist course. Prior to it, I was not aware of all this. I was more instinctive."

"You were being selfish then. You should have, for once, thought of me. I had nobody else and you were the guy in her life. How could you just leave me alone and vanish? I would have been okay if you had come to meet me once and then told me that you would never meet me for real. But you simply absconded. On top of it, Tom also went into hiding. I swear I felt like a criminal.

"Do you know I do everything like Gauri used to do? I walk like her. I talk like her. I talk to her like you do in the night. I talk to the star."

After some brief pause, Itishree continued, "I know I am a girl. I know I am supposed to face the ugliest of things in life. Man made, society made. Not god made. He rather wanted to make something else, but then he ended up creating a woman. He focused on her and then forgot to focus on men. So he gave all of the powers to the woman. Not the powers to rule or dominate. Rather the powers to tolerate, to absorb, to never succumb, to always fight, to yet be sensitive and sensual. So god focused on women a hell lot. To men, he gave the power to control and that's all. And Neil, you are no more the boy I had known. You are a man now. You are no different. You showed me the control. You came to me when you desired. You left us. You left Gauri and me here. Alone. You left us when you desired."

I heard her. Her words killed me treacherously as I had least expected the impact of those. It was the moment of truth for me. I had no other option but to continue to apologize and learn hard lessons from it. "You take your time and make the decision to forgive me when it is appropriate. But tell me something... how'd you know that I talk to the star, I mean Gauri, every night?"

"Because I have a part of her soul that lives in you. Because I feel her like you do, maybe more."

"So what made you switch your subject to dentistry?"

"I decided I will always do what I deem is right. This is what I loved and hence..."

We continued to talk till college almost got over. Time elapsed. Memories came afresh. Nostalgia hit hard. Initially it was aggressively exhausting. The change of emotions and the exchange of discussions at such a rapid pace with so much poignancy made me realize that humans are similar across. What is attached to us will hurt us upon detachment. Nobody becomes inert or a saint overnight. It is a long drawn process where you become real practical and detached. My purpose was to be happy, be at peace and to give to the society.

After some time, we decided to go to the college road coffee shop. She handed over a few CDs to me and told me that she shall return in a bit. She had gone to get some papers photocopied.

Here, on the laptop, while watching Gauri and Itishree's old videos, I saw a recording that was like a pre recording.

After a few seconds had gone by, it seemed like a speech that she had rehearsed for some occasion.

Wait, what, I said to myself. I listened to it carefully.

There was no element of falseness in the fact that Itishree talked and behaved like Gauri. This was the most recent video. I glanced at the timer, so yeah, it was recorded about a couple of weeks ago.

My dearest viewers, audiences and lovely judges......

Aha, so she was preparing for her contest speech and definitely for Miss India!

She continued to talk and thank and then towards the end, she said,

If I win tonight, and I hope I do, I shall make a star fall from the sky. The star that is only there to make all our wishes come true. If I win tonight, and I hope I do, I shall ask that star to make me meet a boy who took away a part of my soul along. Her soul.

Thank you.

It isn't quite often that you are prepared with your saved reactions in such situations. These are unprecedented. And so are the responses.

I came to Tom's room and asked him to take me around Pune. I asked him to take me to the places where I had spent time with Gauri. That included the college canteen and the library. The sight of the college had changed. I was getting constantly hit with vivid memories. The canteen was named Gauri's Cafe and that moved me further. The day was well spent, as I also reworked towards overcoming my fears. My fears that had been subdued in my subconscious state of mind. We stopped over at one of the pubs on the way back to his room.

"What have you decided with life?"

"Finish the padhai, get a job, and travel places. Havana and Tashkent top my list."

"I am really very happy to see you as Neil once again. After so many years, we are able to spend so much time. I love you my man." Tom tightly hugged me as we raised the toast.

"You know, in the last three years, today I feel I have come out of my shell. I truly believe I built that courage of talking about my past, about my insecurities. That actually makes me stronger and real. I believe with every phase, I achieve something, and at that point, it appears to be the be all and end all. But then, again, there is some learning, and again I feel I have achieved something."

"So true, bhai. Life is all about learning from your experiences or otherwise. But it is never-ending."

"Yeah, I feel that sense of satisfaction now. I am also kind of happy to have been associated with this road safety NGO. Wish to keep contributing so that we don't lose more people in road accidents."

"Such a good thought. I am proud of you. How about fixing your own life?"

"It is fixed now. What else remains?"

"Haven't you noticed in her eyes? The madness she displays. The reaction she has when she sees you."

"Who are you talking about?"

"Dumb head, I am talking about Itishree."

"Tom, are you fuckin' out of your mind? You seem to have lost it completely."

"Neil, you have no idea what you are losing. Think about it. A girl who is Gauri's bestie, who reminds you of her, who looked for you like a maniac all these years. A girl who dumped the contest because she got stressed on seeing you after three years, such a girl will never be found. She is one in a billion."

"But she is not Gauri."

"She is the closest to her."

"What will I tell Gauri? That I am cheating on her by loving her best friend."

"You feel liberated but actually you are still caged in a psychologically warped process. That's not true, Neil. Gauri would love for you to settle down again. She would only be happy."

"I am aware and completely aware that I screwed up with Itishree. I had become so aloof then, Tom, if you remember that I wasn't talking to anyone. There was a pretty long interval and then Dharamshala and Buddhism happened. The gap between me and Itishree only widened and honestly I felt it was way too late for me to get back to her. I know I was a fool that I had asked you to not stay in touch with her. That was a terrible mistake."

Tom got up, looked at me and asked about her.

"But now, when you ask me to think about her like a love in my life, I find that more heinous a crime than what Arya had inflicted upon us. I find these words more ruining than my life itself. I really don't know Tom, what made you say all this. I abhor it."

Tom did not intend to give up. He did not budge from his stand. I could see that in his expressions. Mostly when he knows he has missed the point, he would admit it immediately. Here, he repeated it. The same lines. No change. No add on. No skirting the topic. It was point blank in my face.

I was getting furious. To me it was cheating. I hadn't done it when she was there, I won't do it now. My conscience does not allow and I don't feel a thing for any other girl. Just not. In past three years at college, there was not a single instance when I would have thought about a girl. Well, it has never surprised me. Tom was in know how of this in entirety. He had never asked me in the past about it, then why now. Just because she is Itishree, and is talking and walking like her. That does not mean she is her.

Though, after Gauri it was only Itishree whom I had paid some heed to. Of course I knew she wasn't her, yet I thought about her as some replica. The fact that she was Itishree only comforted me in the true sense. Whatever Tom had spoken to me the previous evening did make me think.

It was not making perfect sense to me, but it was still ringing in my head that Itishree did have a soft corner and that she was kind of emotional about us as I had received a few texts from her quite early in the morning.

Neil, sorry it was my pent up anger. If I said anything rude or uncalled for, then forgive me. I wish to meet you one last time before you leave for Delhi. Thanks – Iti.

Hi Itishree, it is absolutely alright. Let us meet at 6 for coffee. I shall come to your college and then we can leave together.

Honestly, I still did not quite know what was going on. Whether I was too excited about meeting Itishree or was it all about Gauri. I was hell confused. I checked Tom's sleeping levels and it wasn't possible to wake him up. I tried my old trick of talking to the mirror and getting the answers. I was trying it after a long time. Last time when I did anything like this was around my entry to the college. I was confused about the stream of subjects to choose. But then, that was about studies. I know that was the most crucial decision that had appealed to me at eighteen. At twenty-three, it was about a girl, my confusion was around my honesty towards her. The mirror said yes.

With that, I tuned myself into one of my favourite programs on radio mirchi. It was a lovely show where RJ Naved would invite listeners to call in and seek their views on relationships. In my past two attempts, I had been successful.

And now the third one made it too.

"Hello my friend, looks like you are having some tough times in life. I welcome you to my show and you may ask me anything that you would want to know. And let me tell my listeners, if you want to know or ask anything, dial 9830983983 now."

"Hey Naved. My name is Neil. I hope you recognize me. We were in school together. This is about a girl who seems to like me. I am confused as she happens to be my girlfriend's bestie, and my girl is now no more in this world. I am supposed to meet her in the evening for coffee. What do I do?"

"Hey Neil, yeah junior, I remember you quite well. First of all, I am so sorry to hear about your girlfriend. According to me, let the girl confess that she really likes you and then take it forward. What is more important for you is that you genuinely like her and are not trying to find your girlfriend and then get hurt because she is a different person."

Those words of Naved were exactly how Tom had explained to me and how the mirror had answered.

The evening was beautiful. It was the beginning of March. The mild breeze made it all the more pleasant. I stood out in the open and looked up in the sky. I needed to talk to Gauri at length today. I needed to get all my answers firmed up.

"Tell me, Gauri. What is happening to me these days? Why am I behaving like this? Have I moved on from you? Am I cheating you? Why have I started thinking of Itishree when I know she is not you? What is wrong with me, Gauri? Please tell me. I always want your happiness. I know that I don't love her like Itishree. But I do think of her as you. Come on!'

Before I could make any statement further, I saw the shooting star. The star that I would talk to every day, the star that was Gauri had fallen off the sky.

You must be my shooting star
Everything I have wished for is everything you are.

I got my answers. You have been liberated today, Gauri. I have set you free. I shall always love you.

Itishree was dressed in a polka dotted skirt and a nice satin top. It had flowers that made her appear vibrant. Her radiance attracted me at first. She was glowing. I opened the car door for her. Tom had recently bought this sedan and I loved its smooth drive.

"Neil, do you want me to drive?"

"Why do you say so?"

"I know when you and Gauri would go out, she always preferred to be behind the wheels. Hence my itch."

I surrendered to her desire to drive me. She throttled and hit the maximum. I was literally jumping on my seat. Itishree was laughing. I screamed and asked her to stop. She asked me not to worry. I told her that I have already lost Gauri in an accident and how I was supporting this NGO that worked for the cause of safe driving. So there was no way that I would allow her to speed.

"It's okay, Neil. I am driving safely. Yes it's a bit fast, but I am in control."

"I don't want to lose you now."

My voice had depth and my eyes carried expressions that Itishree did not want to miss. She returned to the passenger seat and let me drive.

"Neil, thank you for telling me that I am important."

She kept looking at me. I knew she was constantly checking me out, however I pretended I wasn't aware. In this particular situation, even Itishree now knew that I had some feelings for her. It was only a matter of time that we would take this forward.

I was also aware that a lot can happen over coffee and I thought to myself how stupid I was to be talking in the mirror and confirming with Naved. If there is anything that holds you back in human relationships, especially between a boy and girl, just listen to your heart. And my heart kept telling me that I should not stop today.

"Iti, you have seriously begun to look like Gauri."

"You remember you used to tell me that we talk like each other and that besties begin to behave in the same manner. It isn't new that way. Having grown together, we would be doing same things repeatedly. The habits also remained common. After we lost her, I became more conscious. That is when I kept my hair like her and even a bit of make-up meant no harm. That kept me going."

"And you have been through a lot too. Sorry I wasn't there for you."

"We both did, Neil. The only difference was that you left the place and objects behind that would remind you of her. Whereas I lived with those things every single day and night."

I looked into her eyes and watched her lips carefully as she spoke. She held my hand instantly and within a few minutes, asked me what was going on in my mind about the future.

"I will study and then get a job. That's all."

"And what about me? Will you leave me alone, again?"

That statement of hers hit the bottom of my heart. That line sent me goose bumps because I wasn't quite used to such love now. When Itishree said that, I looked clueless. I mean, I was thinking how to say and what to say, so as to not appear like a fool again. Anyway, I had committed so many blunders in the past.

I got closer to Itishree and asked her to smile. She was blushing.

"Iti, tell me what you want. Tell me all."

"It is better I hear it from you, Neil. I have said and done enough already. It becomes important for you to take this to the next level," she said with an expression that only meant it was my turn.

"Okay, Iti. I would love to have you in my life. But I want to ask you a few things, so that I am clear from my heart. I do not want to hide anything from you. May I?"

"When have I stopped you from asking anything? Go on..." she said dismissively.

"You know everything about me. Everything. I would be a fool if I tell you how much I loved Gauri and what she had meant to me and how I only could think of her. I never moved on from her. Not even in the wildest of my imagination. When Tom asked me what I wish to do in life, we had a similar discussion. Okay, let me stop beating about the bush. All I want to tell you is that I see my Gauri in you. Precisely the reason why I wish to take my life forward with you. Tell me if there is anything wrong with that."

"Not at all. In humans, we see our reflection and that is how we connect with those people. Does that make us selfish? The answer is no. When two humans fall in love, they become successful because their love is with the soul and not the body. That is why even when Gauri is not with us, you love her because you fell in love with her soul. Also Neil, I want to tell you something. Can you come with me?"

Itishree took me to the terrace of the coffee shop. We could see the entire view of Pune from the terrace of the twentieth floor. She stood on the side and looked into my eyes. She had something to tell and I had a lot to read from her mind. I was able to build that connect with her. The vibes were positive.

"Iti, what do you wish to say?"

"Ssshhhh...Gauri."

"Gauri, as in?"

"Call me Gauri."

"What do you mean?"

"I have applied for my name change. I wish to be your Gauri for the rest of your life."

My world stopped moving that particular moment. What she said shook me. I was completely taken aback. A girl, who had lost her best buddy, who was more than her sister, lost her friends who she considered to be with her, looked for me for all these years, got into the skin of Gauri and now even renamed herself as Gauri, stood right before me. She had already elevated herself and showed what selflessness and love is all about.

Who am I? What is my worth? I realized I was nobody.

"I am sorry, Iti. I just messed up in my life. Now, when I look at you, I feel I must have done some good karmas that I found you."

"And I promise you Neil, now and for the rest of our life, I shall last forever. We would never talk about the past. I will never ask you anything that makes your situation tough. Think of me like Gauri and no different; that is one promise you have to make in return."

"I do. I love you, Gauri."

Epilogue

Gauri and I got married after four years. We moved to Delhi and Gauri started practicing Dentistry while I moved to an American MNC. There was no news of Arya. The hearsay was that she had left India. Tom and Jerry also shifted to Delhi. They all are leading their happy lives together.

Dhanya and Paul broke up after a year of the wedding. Dhanya and I did not remain in touch for several years but when I met her, I was shocked to know about a few things.

One day, a letter arrived at my house. It was written in blood. That was scary.

The signature read: *Love, Isabella.*

Upcoming title by the same author

All You Need is Love
*The climactic third part of the
'Messed Up!' trilogy*

Neil and Gauri travel to Cuba to celebrate their tenth wedding anniversary, leaving behind their four-year-old daughter Neelakashi with Tom and Mehr. They never return from their vacation.

Find out what happened to the couple deeply in love in this concluding part of the trilogy. A spine-chilling romance thriller, this book shall make you love it.